PALE HORSE

RUSSIAN AND EAST EUROPEAN STUDIES

Jonathan Harris, Editor

PALE HORSE

Boris Savinkov

A NOVEL OF REVOLUTIONARY RUSSIA

TRANSLATED BY MICHAEL R. KATZ

WITH AN INTRODUCTION BY OTTO BOELE

University of Pittsburgh Press

Published by the University of Pittsburgh Press, Pittsburgh, Pa., 15260

Manufactured in the United States of America
Printed on acid-free paper
10 9 8 7 6 5 4 3 2 1

Cataloging-in-Publication data is avialable from the Library of Congress

ISBN 13: 978-0-8229-6570-1
ISBN 10: 0-8229-6570-4

Cover art: Photo collage of a horse skull and Ivan Kaliaev. The photo of Kaliaev was taken right after he was arrested for the assassination of Grand Duke Sergei Alexandrovich.

Cover design: Alex Wolfe

CONTENTS

NOTE ON THE TRANSLATION

THE TEXT CHOSEN FOR THIS TRANSLATION is the uncensored version published in 1913 by M. A. Tumanov in Nice, France, under the author's pseudonym V. Ropshin.

INTRODUCTION

—

Otto Boele

ON MAY 4, 2017, PRESIDENT VLADIMIR PUTIN unveiled a cross-shaped monument on Senate Square in the Moscow Kremlin, exactly on the spot where more than a century earlier Grand Duke Sergei Alexandrovich, an uncle of the tsar, had been killed in a bomb attack. A copy of the original monument, which the Bolsheviks had torn down only weeks after their seizure of power, the newly erected cross was, according to the president, an important reminder. It would make people remember the price that Russia had paid for the mutual hatred and discord of the late imperial period, as well as appreciate the need to preserve national unity in the future. The killing of the grand duke in February 1905 had led to violence and chaos, Putin assured his audience, but the return of the monument was a sign of hope as well as atonement, showing that "in the end truth and justice always prevail."[1]

1. The transcript and video of Putin's speech can be accessed on the Kremlin's official website. "Otkrytie pamiatnika velikomu kniaz'iu Sergeiu Aleksandrovichu," March 4, 2017, accessed November 29, 2017, http://kremlin.ru/events/president/news/54447.

Together the restoration of the monument and the ceremony accompanying its unveiling form a striking example of the "memory politics" that the Kremlin is currently pursuing. The revolution, once a heroic chapter in Russian history that provided the nation with a glorious founding myth, is now officially regarded as a tragic error, as is any form of resistance against "legitimate" regimes, be it in Russia or abroad. Although the grand duke was killed at the beginning of what Soviet historians used to call the "failed revolution" of 1905, in his speech Putin did not specifically mention any of the three revolutions that took place between 1905 and 1917.[2] Instead he spoke of "dramatic events," "civil strife," and a "genuine national catastrophe," as if encouraging his listeners to regard the early twentieth century as a prolonged *smuta,* a period of "troubles" that had nearly destroyed the very idea of Russian statehood.

The grand duke's violent death and its assumed consequences for the Russian Empire look even more dramatic if we consider that Putin refers to the grand duke's killer as "*a terrorist*," as if he were an anonymous agent, possibly a lone wolf. Yet Grand Duke Sergei's killer did not operate on his own; the assassination was the result of well-coordinated teamwork and meticulous planning. Nor did the bomb thrower go down in Russian history as the nameless nonentity that features in Putin's speech. On the contrary, Ivan Kaliaev (1877–1905) is doubtless one of the most famous Russian revolutionaries who inspired dozens of writers to produce a story, a play, or a few lines of poetry, quite often in support of the assassination. In Soviet times at least fifteen cities had one or more streets named after Kaliaev; even today, more than twenty-five years after the breakup of the Soviet Union, only a handful of them have been renamed.

How could a Russian terrorist become so famous and indeed so popular? A tentative answer to that question is the well-known

2. The "three revolutions" are the "failed" Revolution of 1905, the February Revolution of 1917, which led to the tsar's abdication, and the October Revolution of 1917.

adage that "one man's terrorist is another man's freedom fighter."[3] Kaliaev qualified as the latter in the eyes of many Russian contemporaries who abhorred the political oppression and police violence by which the autocracy tried to retain its power. Yet another decisive factor was Kaliaev's good fortune of having an authoritative hagiographer. Without the writing of his friend and fellow terrorist Boris Savinkov, Kaliaev's fame might have been considerably less secure. Savinkov's *Memoirs of a Terrorist*, which has been translated into many languages, describes in great detail the assassination of several top officials, including the grand duke. As early as 1906, only a year after Kaliaev had been arrested and hanged, Savinkov published a very personal essay to honor the memory of his friend, emphasizing not only his dedication to the cause but also his meekness and spiritual contrition over the very act of killing.[4] All of this helped establish Kaliaev's reputation as a revolutionary martyr and a "noble" terrorist in the service of freedom and justice.[5]

Boris Savinkov's novel *Pale Horse* (1909) is essentially another account of the assassination of the grand duke. The main characters can easily be traced to their real-life prototypes, including Kaliaev and Savinkov himself; discussions between the narrator and the party leadership echo genuine controversies that were splitting the Socialist Revolutionary Party (SRP) in whose name the killings were carried out. And yet, when the novel appeared on the pages of the émigré journal *Russian Thought*, it caused outrage and shock.

3. The origin of this saying is contentious. In quoting it I rely on Charles Townshend's *Terrorism: A Very Short Introduction*, 2nd ed. (Oxford: Oxford University Press, 2011), 5.

4. Boris Savinkov, "Iz vospominanii ob Ivane Kaliaeve," in *To chego ne bylo: Roman, povesti, rasskazy, ocherki, stikhotvoreniia*, by Boris Savinkov (V. Ropshin) (Moscow: Sovremennik, 1992), 120–29.

5. Viktor Chernov, the main theoretician of the Socialist Revolutionary Party, described Ivan Kaliaev as "ebullient and direct, a thoughtful enthusiast with a big heart and of uncommon depth. All his words and gestures bore the stamp of something otherworldly." Chernov, *Pered burei. Vospominaniia* (New York: Izdatel'stvo imeni Chekhova, 1953), 188.

Rather than discussing the legitimacy of terrorism in terms of tactics and pragmatism, as had been customary before the bloody events of 1905, *Pale Horse* seemed to focus entirely on the moral complexities of the terrorist's craft.[6] In so doing it not only raised the issue of political violence to a more philosophical, "Dostoevskian" level; for many observers on the left and the Socialist Revolutionaries (SRs) in particular, the novel diminished the lofty aura of the terrorists and damaged the revolutionary movement as a whole. Arguably more than any other fictional text published around this time, *Pale Horse* seriously undermined Russia's "mythology of the underground,"[7] that overarching narrative of political resistance and heroic self-sacrifice through which the left-wing opposition preferred to imagine itself as a tight-knit community of selfless freedom fighters.

Reading *Pale Horse* exclusively in the context of the revolutionary movement and its post-1905 crisis would be insufficient to appreciate the Savinkov phenomenon, however. Apart from masterminding terrorist attacks and fighting the Bolsheviks after the Revolution, Savinkov entertained close contacts with some of the figureheads of Russian modernism, who exposed him to the neoromantic mythmaking with which Russia's fin-de-siècle culture has so often been associated. While providing an exhaustive account of Savinkov's checkered life and literary oeuvre is beyond the scope of this introduction, the discussion below will touch upon both in order to show how his life and work often merged and how the author became indistinguishable from the literary persona he created in *Pale Horse.* Presented as a terrorist's authentic "inside" story, the novel is therefore also an example of what is usually referred to as "life creation": the fashioning of one's life according to the principles of artistic creation, as well as the intentional blurring

6. Daniel Beer, "The Morality of Terror: Contemporary Responses to Political Violence in Boris Savinkov's *The Pale Horse* (1909) and *What Never Happened* (1912)," *Slavonic and East European Review* 85, no. 1 (Jan. 2007): 25–27.

7. M. Mogil'ner, *Mifologiia podpol'nogo cheloveka* (Moscow: Novoe literaturnoe obozrenie, 1999), 41–66.

of the boundaries between art and life.[8] A terrorist, a vice-minister of war in the provisional government under Alexander Kerensky, and a political émigré, Savinkov was simultaneously a writer, a poet, and, above all, the creator of his own eventful life.

Early Years

Boris Viktorovich Savinkov was born in Kharkiv in 1879 and brought up in Warsaw, where his father was appointed a district justice of the peace shortly after the assassination of Tsar Alexander II.[9] His mother, Sof'ia Savinkova (née Iaroshenko), with whom he would remain close throughout his life, was an aspiring playwright who instilled in her children—three sons and three daughters—a love for the arts, in particular literature. Young Boris had a preference for the adventure novels of Sir Walter Scott and Mayne Reid,[10] but as an adolescent he was also well read in the Russian classics. Dostoevsky and Lermontov counted among his favorite authors, a predilection that clearly shines through in *Pale Horse.*

At the first Warsaw Boys' Gimnazium, Savinkov enjoyed the reputation of an exemplary pupil, earning high grades and adhering strictly to the rigorous rules of comportment for which Russia's *gimnaziums* were well known and hated. The tightening of discipline and even firmer surveillance that became customary at institutions of secondary education during the reign of Alexander III did not prevent Savinkov from joining a socialist cell that was operating in his school. Here he befriended Kaliaev (a classmate of

8. On life creation see the excellent edited volume *Creating Life: The Aesthetic Utopia of Russian Modernism*, ed. Irina Paperno and Joan Delaney Grossman (Stanford, CA: Stanford University Press, 1994).
9. For information on Savinkov's life I rely mainly on Richard B. Spence's biography *Boris Savinkov: Renegade on the Left* (Boulder, CO: East European Monographs, 1991).
10. Thomas Mayne Reid (1818–1883) was an Irish American writer of adventure novels.

his older brother Alexander), with whom he would carry out two of the SRs' most sensational assassinations.

After moving to Saint Petersburg to study law in 1897, Savinkov immediately became active in the radical student movement, boosting his revolutionary credentials further by marrying Vera Uspenskaya, daughter of the well-known populist author Gleb Uspensky. He was arrested twice and expelled from university, after which he spent a year abroad. Back in Russia, his freedom proved short-lived; the assassination of minister of education Nikolai Bogolepov—widely despised for having rebellious students conscripted into the army—led to a wave of arrests that finally caught up with Savinkov as well. He was incarcerated for several months in the notorious Peter and Paul Fortress in January 1902 and then sentenced to live under police surveillance in the provincial town of Vologda.

Although Savinkov managed to escape to Switzerland in less than a year, his forced stay in Vologda was to have a lasting impact on his political views and the role he envisioned for himself. Unsatisfied with the political agenda of Lenin's Social Democratic Party for "leaving the agrarian question unresolved,"[11] Savinkov decided to join the SRs, who bet on the Russian peasantry, not the urban proletariat as Marxism dictated. Whether this really was a crucial issue to Savinkov is open to debate. A romantic and a man of action, he seems to have lacked the appetite and the patience for political theory, while his familiarity with the peasantry must have been fairly limited. Above all, he was attracted by the prospect of following in the footsteps of The People's Will, the terrorist group that had killed Alexander II and for which Savinkov was said to harbor deep sympathy.[12] The ultimate trigger to choose the path of terror was the arrest of Grigory Gershuni, the founder of the Combat Organization of the SRs, who had devised the shooting of minister of interior Dmitry Sipiagin in April 1902.[13] This was the

11. Boris Savinkov, "Vospominaniia terrorista," in *Izbrannoe* (Leningrad: Khudozhestvennaia literatura: 1990), 25.

12. Savinkov, "Vospominaniia terrorista," 25.

Combat Organization's first major success and it did much to establish the SRs as one of the regime's most formidable opponents.

Savinkov was eventually recruited by Yekaterina Breshko-Breshkovskaya (1844–1934), the "Grandmother of the Revolution," who visited Vologda twice during Savinkov's exile. A radical populist and a participant in the "going-to-the-people" campaign of the mid-1870s, Breshko-Breshkovskaya was eager to reboot the populist movement by helping to establish the SRs as a formal organization and recruiting new members. Apart from informing Savinkov about Kaliaev's decision to participate in the terror campaign (thereby encouraging him to follow suit), she actually helped him escape to Switzerland, where he was introduced to Evno Azef, the acting chief of the Combat Organization. It was from Azef, who would later be exposed as a double agent, that Savinkov received his first major assignment: coordinating the murder plot against minister of the interior Vyacheslav von Plehve. After months of stalking their intended victim and several abortive attempts, Savinkov and four other combatants (among whom was Kaliaev) finally succeeded in executing their plan. On July 15, 1904, Yegor Sazonov, dressed as a railway worker, hurled a bomb at von Plehve's carriage, killing both the minister and his coachman.

Three Martyrs and a Voyeur

Our twenty-first-century perception of terrorism is inevitably shaped by the events of 9/11, suicide bombings in the Middle East, and the more recent attacks in Europe by Islamic State, but, as Anthony Anemone has pointed out, in late imperial Russia "advocates of political violence construed legitimate targets quite nar-

13. Savinkov, "Vospominaniia terrorista," 25.
14. Anthony Anemone, "Introduction," in *Just Assassins: The Culture of Terrorism in Russia*, ed. Anthony Anemone (Evanston, IL: Northwestern University Press, 2010), 5.

rowly."[14] Potential victims were members of the imperial family and government officials, whose assassination would confuse the authorities, the SRs believed, and destabilize the entire regime.[15] The modern practice of hitting "soft targets" among the civilian population was alien to the SRP, even if certain factions eventually resorted to more indiscriminate forms of violence using increasingly heavier explosives. As a shocking example of some terrorists' lack of concern for human life, Anna Geifman adduces the attempted assassination of prime minister Piotr Stolypin in his villa on Aptekarsky Island by three socialist revolutionary "maximalists" in August 1906 that left twenty-seven people killed and over sixty injured.[16]

In 1903, when Savinkov and Kaliaev had just joined the Combat Organization, terrorists were still widely perceived as martyrs, exceptional men and women prepared to sacrifice their young lives in exchange for that of a considerably older governor or minister. By getting killed in the attack or receiving the death penalty the assassin was believed to atone for the bloodshed he or she had caused. This romanticized view conveniently ignored the issue of collateral casualties, as well as the fact that some terrorists survived and escaped,[17] but it does illustrate the apparent allure of political violence that many terrorists must have experienced knowing that

15. On the purpose of terror see Beer, "Morality of Terror," 32–33; see also Daniel Brower's essay "Nihilists and Terrorists," in *Times of Trouble: Violence in Russian Literature and Culture*, ed. Marcus C. Levitt and Tatyana Novikov (Madison: University of Wisconsin Press, 2007), 91–102.

16. Anna Geifman, *Thou Shalt Kill: Revolutionary Terrorism in Russia, 1894–1917* (Princeton, NJ: Princeton University Press, 1993), 74.

17. In 1878 Sergei Kravchinsky killed Nikolai Mezentsov, head of Russia's secret police, with a dagger, but managed to escape to England where he became a celebrity, especially after the publication of his *Underground Russia* (1883), in which he offered to the Western reader a "who's who" of Russian terrorists. Egor Sazonov, who threw the fatal bomb that killed von Plehve, was severely wounded, but survived. After his recovery, he was sent to Siberia, where he committed suicide in 1910. On Kravchinsky see Peter Scotto, "The Terrorist as Novelist: Sergei Stepniak," in Anemone, *Just Assassins*, 97–126.

it was exclusively directed at carefully selected representatives of an oppressive regime. Kaliaev's now legendary split-second decision to abort the first attempt on the grand duke's life after noticing that his wife and children were in the carriage with him stemmed, in Kaliaev's own analysis, from the party line as much as from his own moral constraints.[18]

A key element in the mythology of the revolutionary movement, the idea of heroic self-sacrifice was an obsession for some of Savinkov's accomplices, who often insisted on being allowed to throw the first bomb instead of acting as mere backup. This is faithfully depicted in *Pale Horse* when Vanya and Heinrich (in whom one recognizes Kaliaev and Sazonov) dispute each other's right to make the first attempt. The only woman on Savinkov's team, Dora Brilliant, who prepared the bombs for the attacks on von Plehve and the grand duke, was devastated by the impossibility of paying for the assassinations with her own blood. Time and again she asked Savinkov permission to take part in the actual killing, but he never conceded.[19] Smitten by her conscience, she was arrested in 1907 and imprisoned in the Peter and Paul Fortress, where she died two years later.

In his memoirs Savinkov writes warmly about his partners in crime, who, for all their characterological differences, had two things in common: their almost religious faith in the revolution and their fanatical commitment to the terror. The portraits of Brilliant and Sazonov in *Memoirs of a Terrorist* may be somewhat exaggerated, as they appear to be informed by earlier depictions of "unwavering" revolutionaries, but it is certain that they were almost pathologically preoccupied with the terror. In this respect they form a striking contrast with Savinkov, who, most observers agreed, was of

18. Kaliaev as quoted by Savinkov, "Vospominaniia terrorista," 99. Kaliaev's restraint inspired existentialist Albert Camus to write his famous play *The Just Ones* (*Les justes*, 1949).

19. Savinkov, "Vospominaniia terrorista," 48–49.

an entirely different bent.[20] His never-waning egocentrism, as well as the ease with which he would later adopt a more nationalistic rather than a revolutionary agenda, set him apart from the other combatants, some of whom were pious Christians. Although *Pale Horse* is permeated with Christian symbolism, the example of Jesus Christ never seems to have appealed to Savinkov. In the words of Richard Spence: "Like his comrades Sazonov, Brilliant and Kaliaev, Savinkov was willing to kill for the cause, but unlike them he was not particularly interested in dying for it."[21]

Whether Savinkov actually killed is questionable too, as he had a different role than the rank-and-file members of the Combat Organization. Being in charge of the operations, but not an assigned killer, he may have never spilled any blood himself, not even during the revolution or the civil war. Although no one ever felt inclined to question his courage or his willingness to use any of the weapons he was always carrying with him, with regard to death and violence, Savinkov was, as Spence puts it, "basically a voyeur."[22] With its connotations of sexual gratification, the term "voyeur" may seem out of place in this context, and yet it is quite appropriate considering Savinkov's proclivity for the theatrical (of which more below) and his ability to perceive a murder plot "aesthetically"; that is, as something creative that requires planning, deceit, and role play. In this respect, too, he was quite different from his comrades for whom terrorism was an entirely moral dilemma. With a bit of a stretch one could argue that the dividing line between the "martyrs" and the "voyeur" Savinkov replicated the "either/or" oppo-

20. Anatolii Lunacharsky, who headed the People's Commissariat for Education in the late 1910s and 1920s, knew Savinkov well from when they were both serving time in Vologda. In an article published in *Pravda* in September 1924 he acknowledged Savinkov's literary talent, but also emphasized his "petty-bourgeois romanticism." See Anatolii Lunacharskii, "Artist i avantiury," *Pravda*, September 5, 1924.

21. Spence, *Boris Savinkov*, 37.

22. Spence, *Boris Savinkov*, 37.

sition that Søren Kierkegaard described juxtaposing the aesthetic view of life to the ethical one.

After 1905

The assassination of the grand duke in 1905 was the zenith of the Combat Organization's existence and of Savinkov's personal career as a terrorist. Only weeks later the organization was severely weakened by a wave of arrests (mostly Azef's doing); toward the end of the year the Central Committee decided to disband it, despite Savinkov's vehement protests. Although the terror would eventually be resumed and the Combat Organization reinstated, in subsequent years none of the attacks would have the resonance created by the earlier killings. The old method of stalking and covert observation seemed superseded, especially for high-profile targets who were increasingly better protected. Attempts on lower officials were more successful, but these were typically carried out in the provinces by smaller terrorist units or even individuals operating on their own initiative. In addition to an avalanche of "revolutionary expropriations," these uncoordinated attacks on almost anyone remotely associated with the regime did much to discredit the SRs and the revolutionary movement as a whole.

From 1907 until the fall of the monarchy in February 1917 Savinkov spent most of his time in France. In May 1906 he had been arrested in Sevastopol for his supposed involvement in a murder plot against General Nepliuev (which is ironic, as he *was* preparing an attack on Admiral Chukhnin), but he had managed to escape from prison disguised as a soldier and make his way in a small boat across the Black Sea to Romania. Having settled in Paris, Savinkov made many new acquaintances both in political and cultural circles. He was particularly close to the symbolist poet Zinaida Gippius and her husband, Dmitry Merezhkovsky, whom he had met while still in Russia. Under Gippius's mentorship, but with significant input from Merezhkovsky as well, Savinkov started working on *Pale*

Horse. The novel was written simultaneously with the more factual accounts of the assassinations of von Plehve and Grand Duke Sergei that would eventually morph into Savinkov's *Memoirs of a Terrorist.*

That a revolutionary decided to try his hand at a novel is anything but surprising given the crucial role fictional literature played in prerevolutionary Russia. In the absence of a free press, the novel was the vehicle par excellence to convey a subversive message, present inspiring portraits of revolutionary trailblazers, or simply dissect and diagnose Russian society. Having access to *Revolutionary Russia* and other periodicals published abroad, Savinkov did not have to resort to fiction, of course, but literature did offer the prospect of reaching a larger audience and, more importantly, turning his individual experience into something broader. In a way, it was the natural thing to do; some twenty years earlier Sergei Stepniak-Kravchinsky had been quite successful with his novel *The Career of a Nihilist* (also known under the title *Andrei Kozhukhov*), in which the author drew heavily on his own experience as a terrorist and assassin.

Of course, Savinkov's interest in literature was deeper than the mere publication of *Pale Horse* suggests. He was well read in Russian poetry and liked to recite Lermontov and Semion Nadson.[23] Just like Kaliaev, who was nicknamed "the poet," he wrote some quasi-symbolist poetry himself (posthumously published in Paris). As early as in 1903 he had published a story under the pseudonym V. Kanin for which he had received assistance from one no less than Leonid Andreev, then one of Russia's most popular authors.[24] Now, in the relative safety of his Paris apartment, he finally had the chance to take his literary ambitions more seriously and embark on a novel.

23. Semion Nadson (1862–1887), a poet heavily influenced by Lermontov, continued Russian poetry's "civic" tradition in the 1880s. Among the radical left he was one of Russia's most popular poets.

24. Spence, *Boris Savinkov*, 92.

Pale Horse

Written in the form of a diary, *Pale Horse* tells the story of a terrorist leader who arrives in Moscow to coordinate a murder plot against the local governor. Having assumed the identity of a British tourist by the name of George O'Brien, the hero meets with his accomplices and discusses the details of the assassination with a mixture of cynicism and boredom. Unlike his four comrades who seem to believe in the ideals of the revolution and are prepared to die for it, George feels nothing but indifference and a vague but growing determination to kill his designated target.

"It's always possible to kill," he replies laconically when his deeply religious friend Vanya posits that murder is only permissible if it's committed out of "genuine love." If it doesn't serve a higher purpose and the murderer isn't tormented by deep remorse, "then it's Smerdyakov" and "everything is allowed." Vanya's reference to the killer in Dostoevsky's last novel, *The Brothers Karamazov*, is most revealing with regard to George, who recognizes no moral laws and finally commits a murder in an entirely personal affair. By shooting the husband of his mistress he turns Vanya's words about "killing out of genuine love" into a travesty that leaves him to ponder the deeper significance of his deeds. "Why did I kill? What did I accomplish by death? Yes, I believed that one could kill. But now I feel sad: I killed not only him [the husband of his mistress]; I also killed love." Agonized by an inner void that he can no longer ignore, George sees no other solution but suicide.

Russian literature wasn't short of one-dimensional revolutionaries and even terrorists fighting autocracy or otherwise busy creating a better, more just society. Bazarov, Rakhmetov, and Kozhukhov, to name only a few,[25] were designed—or so construed

25. Bazarov is the main character in Turgenev's novel *Fathers and Children* (1861); Rakhmetov is a revolutionary superman in Chernyshevsky's *roman à thèse, What Is to Be Done?* (1863). Finally, Kozhukhov is the hero in Stepniak-Kravchinky's novel *Career of a Nihilist.*

by radical critics—as adumbrating a new era, the era of "New People," in which social justice and prosperity for all would prevail. Together with a few other novels, *Pale Horse* broke with this tradition.[26] It was, in Aileen Kelly's words, a "savage demystification of the monolithic hero,"[27] an onslaught on a behavioral ideal that leftist literature had been promoting for years. George not only kills in his own interest; he also expresses sincere doubts about the ends that usually justify the means: "I don't believe in paradise on earth; I don't believe in paradise in heaven." He is even more direct in his last conversation with Andrei Petrovich, a member of the Central Committee, when he declines a new assignment with the words: "Why kill?" Andrei Petrovich's amazed reaction ("What do you mean?") serves to illustrate George's estrangement from the party, but ultimately invites us to question the rationale behind the terror itself: why kill indeed?

If this is really the novel's intended message, are we dealing with the confession of a repenting terrorist? This is how many critics preferred to interpret *Pale Horse*, especially when it came to light that it was Savinkov who was hiding behind the pseudonym of V. Ropshin. In the view of conservative and liberal opinion makers the novel signaled the radical intelligentsia's "moral bankruptcy," which had revealed itself after the failure of 1905. Starting with Turgenev's

26. The most important candidate in this respect is Mikhail Artsybashev's "pornographic" novel *Sanin* (1907), whose eponymous hero was also construed as an ex-revolutionary "betraying" the revered traditions of the Russian intelligentsia. In a combined review of *Sanin* and *Pale Horse*, socialist critic Vladimir Kranikhfel'd even used the name Sanin-George to emphasize that both characters embodied the same "I-want-and-therefore-have-the-right-to" mentality of Russia's budding capitalism under Prime Minister Stolypin. Kranikhfel'd, "Literaturnye otkliki. Stavka na sil'nykh," *Sovremmenyi mir,* 1909, 5, 78. For a more extensive discussion of the strong-willed hero in turn-of-the-century literature see Otto Boele, *Erotic Nihilism in Late Imperial Russia: The Case of Mikhail Artsybashev's Sanin* (Madison: Wisconsin University Press, 2009).

27. Aileen Kelly, "Self-Censorship and the Russian Intelligentsia, 1905–1914," *Slavic Review* 46, no. 2 (Summer 1987): 201.

epoch-making nihilist Bazarov, radicals had developed a worldview in which the elementary notion of "truth" was always subordinated to a narrowly defined political agenda.[28] To some, Savinkov's novel was therefore a hopeful indication that the radical left was sobering up from its delusions and becoming more susceptible to ideas from outside its own environment. The promise of the hero's suicide at the end of his diary seemed to provide the necessary poetic justice.

The idea that *Pale Horse* could and, perhaps, should be read as an authentic confession was most emphatically promulgated by Merezhkovsky, who had closely monitored the writing of *Pale Horse* and, of course, knew that Savinkov was the real author. In a long-winded review he hailed the novel as the "most Russian book" to have been written after the immortal works of Tolstoy and Dostoevsky, not "so much because of the book itself, but because of what is behind it."[29] Here Merezhkovsky in all probability had in mind not only Savinkov's very real experience with terrorism but also the lengthy discussions that he and Gippius had had with Savinkov on the moral justification of violence. According to Gippius, Savinkov was tormented by the blood he had spilled. He even confessed that each time he killed, it felt as if he were getting killed himself.[30]

While it is impossible to establish how sincere Savinkov was in these discussions, one should not conclude too easily that it was genuine compunction—or compunction alone—that inspired him to write *Pale Horse*. Not only did he never abandon the idea of waging terror against his opponents, be they tsarist officials or Bol-

28. See in particular the essay "Filosofskaia istina i intelligentskaia pravda," Nikolai Berdiaev's contribution to the infamous collection of essays *Vekhi* (Signposts), which was published in 1909. *Vekhi. Intelligentsiia v Rossii* (Moscow: Molodaia gvardiia, 1991), 30.

29. D. S. Merezhkovsky, "Kon' blednyi," in *Ne mir, no mech* (Moscow: AST, 2000), 495.

30. Zinaida Gippius, "Dmitrii Merezhkovii," in *Sobranie sochinenii*, T. 6 (Zhivye litsa. Vospominaniia. Stikhotvoreniia), (Moscow: Russkaia kniga, 2002), 320.

sheviks; in the same year that his novel was published, he became the head of the Combat Organization, which he would run for over two years. This paradox leads Lynn Ellen Patyk to doubt whether the novel can possibly be read as a moral critique of terrorism or, even more generally, as a polemical statement.[31] Pointing out that Savinkov started his literary and revolutionary careers virtually in tandem, she argues that *Pale Horse* is best viewed as "the first literary installment of Ropshin-Savinkov's self-mythologization."[32] Profoundly influenced by romantic poets such as Byron and Ler montov, Savinkov embraced a model of self-authorship that enabled him to transform his life into a work of art playing out his "tormented consciousness" in literary salons and investing his fictional hero with autobiographical elements.

For Gippius and Merezhkovsky Savinkov appeared to be a guilt-ridden, highly intriguing individual possessed by a "fatal mystery" that they interpreted not in a Byronic but a Christian key. In their perception Savinkov resembled Dostoevsky's antiheroes Raskolnikov and Stavrogin, who subconsciously seek salvation but cannot give up their romantic individualism. Gippius herself provided a positive counterimage to the "revolutionary aesthete": the ideal terrorist who, while committing a terrible sin, acts out of love and sacrifices himself, thereby performing a "Christian deed of heroic martyrdom." It is this image of the ideal terrorist that made it to Savinkov's novel in the character of Vanya, the pious, conscience-stricken terrorist. Patyk urges us to acknowledge the literary origins of the character and not to assume a one-to-one correspondence between Vanya and his alleged prototype, Ivan Kaliaev. As Patyk puts it: "Savinkov and his fictions were in fact saturated with literariness." Rather than articulating genuine repentance, *Pale Horse* is a testimony to Savinkov's obsession with the

31. Lynn Ellen Patyk, "The Byronic Terrorist: Boris Savinkov's Literary Self-Mythologization," in Anemone, *Just Assassins*, 165.

32. Patyk, "Byronic Terrorist," 165.

models of literary romanticism and his sensitivity to his symbolist friends' life-creating pursuits.

The *Baba* and the Terrorist

Although the author behind the pseudonym V. Ropshin was not Gippius herself, as some critics had conjectured, her role in the genesis of *Pale Horse* and its publication was indeed of key importance. In the same year that the novel was published in the January issue of the émigré periodical *Russian Thought*, it came out as a separate edition in Russia, albeit with significant cuts made by the self-censoring editors of publisher *Shipovnik*.[33] Gippius, who had plugged the novel and negotiated the adjustments more or less on her own, tried to soothe Savinkov by pointing out that the removal of certain historical details, to which the author had attached great significance, did not diminish the novel's veracity. What mattered was not "how it has really been," but "how it *could* have been. This is where art emerges," she wrote to him.[34]

Earlier Gippius had also tried to have a say in what is seemingly the plot's most puzzling aspect: George's somewhat unlikely romance with Elena, a sensual woman from well-to-do circles who enjoys having an affair with a dangerous terrorist but refuses to leave the military officer to whom she is married. For Savinkov, who was married twice, had three legal children, and enjoyed the reputation of a womanizer, carnal desire and promiscuity did not necessarily discredit his hero—quite the contrary, if we consider his Byronic-Lermontovian lineage. Gippius, however, in true symbolist fashion, conceived of erotic love as something destructive, even diabolic if it didn't bring closer the ideal of androgyny and only served the

33. Of this self-censored edition a mere 3,200 copies were printed. See E. I. Goncharova's comments in *Pis'ma Merezhkovskikh k Borisu Savinkovu*, ed. E. I. Goncharova (Saint Petersburg: Pushkinskii dom, 2009), 154.

34. Gippius to Savinkov, February 6, 1909, in Goncharova, *Pis'ma*, 157.

continuation of the human species. Hence her conclusion that the novel became somehow "distorted" the moment Savinkov "injected a positive element into the question of sexual love." Merezhkovsky chimed in, pointing out that the Elena aspect was the weakest part of the novel: "You suffer from a naïve sort of romanticism with regard to Elena. It's as if not only the hero, but you too are in love with her."[35] In the end, Gippius reconciled herself with Elena's place in the novel, not because the character had been substantially altered (she remained a *baba* and a "chicken"[36]) but because, in Gippius's analysis, the hero ultimately understands that she is not right for him (*ne to*). When George shoots her husband, he quickly loses interest in her and the relationship is over: "I have no bitterness for Elena. It's as if my fatal shot burned up my love."

If for Gippius and Merezhkovsky the character of the highly feminine Elena was problematic, from a literary-historical perspective her presence in *Pale Horse* is anything but surprising. Quite a few nineteenth-century Russian novels feature a Westernized hero who seeks the love of a distinctly Russian woman but is frustrated by a third character representing the state. Based on the rivalry of two masculine adversaries (the *intelligent* versus the authorities), this recurring plot reflects the problematic status of the alienated intelligentsia who "courts" Russia by studying and enlightening its people, but never succeeds in winning her love. While in the work of Alexander Blok and Andrei Bely the metaphor becomes more explicit and the fictitious female character is replaced by the image of Russia as unattainable bride,[37] *Pale Horse*

35. Merezhkovsky to Savinkov, May 1908, in Goncharova, *Pis'ma*, 112.

36. Gippius uses the words "baba" (uncultured woman from the lower strata of society) and "kuritsa" (chicken) to express her dismay with the "overly" feminine character of Elena.

37. Yurii Lotman was the first to observe this pattern in nineteenth-century Russian prose. See his "Siuzhetnoe prostranstvo v russkom romane XIX stoletiia," in *Izbrannye stat'i v trekh tomakh* (Tallinn: Aleksandra, 1993), T. III, 98. A far more developed discussion can be found in Ellen Rutten's *Unattainable Bride Russia: Gendering Nation, State, and Intelligentsia in Russian Intellectual Culture* (Evanston, IL: Northwestern University Press, 2010), 39–40.

shows a similarly gendered constellation of characters and conflicts with George's political struggle against the existing order having a parallel in his duel with Elena's husband. Although George is, technically speaking, successful in both confrontations (the governor and his amorous opponent are killed), the ultimate goal remains unattainable. Consequently, rather than "distorting" the novel, as Gippius claimed, the inclusion of Elena shows how much *Pale Horse* continues the nineteenth-century tradition of presenting an amorous intrigue between a male *intelligent* and a Russian woman as a metaphor for the social divide between the intelligentsia and the "masses."

Revolution, Civil War, and Death

Savinkov's second novel, *What Never Happened* (*To chego ne bylo*, 1912), is a longer and more ambitious work with an omniscient narrator telling the story of three brothers who all die in the name of the revolution. Describing, among other things, the Battle of Tsushima, the bloody exploits of a "flying squad" of terrorists, and the betrayal and exposure of a double-dealing agent, the novel contains far more violence than *Pale Horse*, thus conjuring up a captivating image of the anarchy and chaos during roughly the years 1904–1908. In addition to presenting the revolutionary movement as lying in shambles, the novel offers highly unflattering portraits of "phrasemongering" party leaders no longer in touch with reality. One of the few exceptions is Andrei Bolotov, the second of the three brothers (like Savinkov himself), who comes to the conviction that "only he has the right to talk about murder who commits murder himself and about death who himself is prepared to die."[38] On these grounds he ignores the Central Committee's orders not to engage in combat himself and decides to support a spontaneous revolt of Moscow workers. Even if Andrei Bolotov's

38. "To chego ne bylo," in Savinkov, *To chego ne bylo*, 258.

determination to join the action could be interpreted as a desperate attempt to restore the monolithic hero to his former glory, his embitterment and estrangement from the party indicate otherwise.

Predictably, among the radical left, particularly in the ranks of the SRs, *What Never Happened* created a scandal that made the fuss over Savinkov's debut novel pale. But apart from blackening Savinkov's former comrades and discrediting the revolutionary movement as a whole, the novel also seemed to articulate a militant kind of chauvinism that placed its author on the right of the political spectrum. The deepest emotion inciting the oldest of the three fictional brothers to support the revolution is indignation over Russia's humiliating defeat against Japan. Alexander Bolotov comes to the conclusion that it would only be fitting if he, an officer of the Russian navy and a former POW, sacrificed himself for the revolution, thus "taking revenge for Port Arthur and Tsushima."[39] Wandering through the Kremlin, he experiences an epiphany of "Russianness": "Only here, in peasant Moscow, in the city of tar, oilcloth, miracle-working icons, and crushed barricades, did he feel with all this heart that he was Russian, that he was connected to Russia by blood."[40]

While these are only the words of a fictional character, it is true that at the eve of the First World War Savinkov seemed to care less about the revolution than about Russia as a nation. He welcomed the outbreak of the war and even called for the suspension of all revolutionary activities with a view to Russia's military needs. Working as a freelance war correspondent in France and Belgium, Savinkov proved himself an unabashed patriot and a supporter of the Allied cause. After his return to Russia in April 1917 he continued in a similar vein as a military commissar on the Galician front boosting men's morale and urging them not to give in to the anti-

39. "To chego ne bylo," 470.

40. "To chego ne bylo," 470.

war propaganda of the Bolsheviks. For two months he was acting minister of war in Kerensky's provisional government.

During the last years of his life Savinkov was obsessed with one thing: to oust the Bolsheviks and seize power himself. None of the many political alliances he forged in war-torn Russia or abroad were successful, however, and the fact that he supported and openly admired Alexander Kolchak (chief commander of the White Army) or even tried to win Benito Mussolini over to his cause, testifies to the desperation he must have felt, as well as to his fascination with "strong" leaders. According to Spence, Savinkov was more of a "power-seeker than a true revolutionary and more an authoritarian than a democrat."[41]

Eventually, Savinkov decided to return to Soviet Russia knowing that he would be immediately arrested and convicted for his contrarevolutionary activities. Like other emigrants he may have hoped to join the Bolsheviks once their defeat proved impossible and that he could be of use to them as a one-time but now "remorseful" opponent with an expertise in conspiracy and covert warfare. It is indeed remarkable, and probably telling, that while being imprisoned and interrogated by Felix Dzerzhinsky, head of the Cheka,[42] Savinkov was allowed to continue writing and that his stories were published. One of them, "Imprisoned," is about a contrarevolutionary whose self-aggrandizement and cowardice are negatively contrasted with the correctness and honesty of the Cheka officers interrogating him.

Savinkov died a prisoner on May 7, 1925. While being escorted to his cell after a stroll, he seized the opportunity to throw himself out of a window on the fifth floor of the Liubianka prison. This, at least, is the official version, but rumors about Savinkov being pushed spread almost immediately after his death was announced. The third and most unlikely version holds that the suicide attempt

41. Spence, *Boris Savinkov*, 374.

42. The Extraordinary Commission to Combat Counterrevolution and Sabotage.

was a fake, designed by the Cheka or Savinkov himself, and that he lived well beyond 1925. In Russia, with its rich tradition of pretenders and conspiracy theories, such speculation is usually restricted to the imperial family, but the dissemination of such rumors about Boris Savinkov stands as a monument to his reputation for disguise and deceit.

PALE HORSE

Boris Savinkov

PART ONE

And I looked, and behold a pale horse: and his name that sat on him was Death, and Hell followed with him.

Book of Revelation 6:8

. . . he that hateth his brother is in darkness and walketh in darkness, and knoweth not whither he goeth, because that darkness hath blinded his eyes.

1 John 2:11

MARCH 6

Last evening I arrived in Moscow. It is much the same. Crosses glitter on churches, sleigh runners squeak on the snow. There's frost in the mornings and patterns on the windows; the monastery bells summon people to church. I love Moscow. It feels like home.

I have a passport with the red stamp of the English king and the signature of Lord Lansdowne.[1] It says that I am a British subject named George O'Brien undertaking a journey to Turkey and Russia. I am registered as a "tourist" with the Russian police.

In the hotel everything is so familiar it bores me to death: the doorman in his blue jacket, the gilded mirrors, and the carpets. There's a worn sofa in my room and dusty curtains. And three kilos

---

1. Edward VII (1841–1910) was king of the United Kingdom and the British Dominions and emperor of India from 1901 until his death in 1910. Henry Charles Keith Petty-Fitzmaurice, fifth Marquess of Lansdowne (1845–1927), was the British foreign secretary from 1900 to 1905.

of dynamite under the table. I've brought them from abroad. The dynamite reeks of the pharmacy and I get headaches at night.

I'm going to take a walk around Moscow today. It's dark on the boulevards, and it's snowing lightly. A clock is chiming somewhere. I'm all alone, there's not a soul out. Before me lies peaceful life, forgotten people. In my heart the sacred words resound: "I will give you the morning star."[2]

MARCH 8

Erna has blue eyes and thick braids. She clings to me timidly and says, "You love me a little, don't you?"

Some time ago she gave herself to me like a queen: she didn't demand anything in return and didn't expect anything. And now, like a beggar, she asks for love. I look out the window at the snow-covered square.

I say, "Look at the untouched snow."

She lowers her head and remains silent.

Then I say, "Yesterday I was in Sokolniki. The snow's even purer there. It's rose-colored. And the shadows of the birch trees are blue."

In her eyes I read, *You went there without me.*

"Listen," I say again, "have you ever been in the Russian countryside?"

She replies, "No."

"Well, in the early spring, when the grass is already turning green and the snowdrops are beginning to bloom in the woods, there's still snow in the ravines. It's strange: white snow and white flowers. Have you ever seen it? No? You didn't understand? No?"

She whispers, "No."

And I think about Elena.

2. "And I will give him the morning star," Book of Revelation 2:28.

MARCH 9

The governor-general lives in his palace.[3] He's surrounded by spies and guards. A double barrier of soldiers and immodest glances.

We're a small group: five people. Fyodor, Vanya, Heinrich—all dressed as carriage drivers. They follow him constantly and report their observations to me. Erna's a chemist. She will make the bombs.

I sit at a table in my room and draw up plans for our route. I try to reconstruct his life. He and I greet guests together in the entrance hall of his house. We stroll together in the garden, behind the gate. We hide together at night. We pray together to God.

I saw him today. I was waiting for him on Tverskaya Street. I wandered for a long time along the frozen sidewalk. Evening was approaching; the weather was freezing. I had already lost all hope. All of a sudden the officer on the corner waved his gloved hand. The policemen stood at attention; detectives rushed about. The street fell silent.

A carriage came rushing past. Black horses. A coachman with a red beard. The door handles were curved, the spokes of the wheels yellow. His guards followed the sleigh.

I could hardly make out his face as he raced by. He didn't see me: for him I was part of the street.

I felt happy and returned home slowly.

MARCH 10

When I think about him I feel neither hatred nor malice. Nor do I have any pity. I'm indifferent toward him. But I want his death. I know: he must be killed. It's necessary for the terror and for the

3. A reference to Grand Duke Sergei Alexandrovich of Russia (1857–1905), the fifth son of Alexander II. He was an influential figure during the reigns of his brother Alexander III and his nephew Nicholas II. Targeted by the Social Revolutionary Combat Organization, he was assassinated by a terrorist bomb at the Kremlin.

revolution. I believe that "might makes right."[4] If I could, I would kill all the superiors and rulers. I don't want to be a slave. I don't want anyone to be a slave.

They say one shouldn't commit murder. Furthermore, they say that it's all right to kill a minister, but not a revolutionary. And they also say the opposite.

I don't know why one shouldn't commit murder. And I shall never understand why it's right to kill in the name of freedom but wrong to kill in the name of autocracy.

I remember when I was on a hunting trip for the first time. The fields of buckwheat were ripening, there were cobwebs everywhere, and the forest was silent. I stood at the edge of it, near a road pitted by the rain. At times the birch trees whispered, yellow leaves flew past. I waited. Suddenly there was an unusual rustling in the grass. A rabbit came running out of the bushes like a small grey bundle, and cautiously sat up on its hind feet. He looked around. Trembling, I raised my gun. The echo resounded through the forest; a puff of grey smoke rose among the birches. The wounded hare struggled on the grass stained with his blood. He whimpered like a baby. I felt sorry for him. I shot him a second time. He fell silent.

At home I forgot all about him immediately. It was as if he had never existed, as if it wasn't me who had deprived him of what was most precious—his life. And I ask myself: why did I find it painful when he cried out? Why did I not feel pain when I killed him for my amusement?

MARCH 11

Fyodor's a blacksmith, a former worker from the Presnya district. He wears blue overalls and a cabby's cap. He sips his tea from a saucer. I say to him, "Were you on the barricades in December?"

"Me? I was sitting in the house."

4. A Russian proverb; literally, "strength will break a straw."

"In which house?"

"At school; that is, the city school."

"What for?"

"I was in reserve. I had two bombs."

"In other words, you didn't fire."

"What do you mean? I did."

"Well, tell me."

He waves his arm. "What of it? The artillery arrived. They began firing at us from cannons."

"What did you do?"

"We did, too. . . . We fired at them from cannons. We made them ourselves at the factory. They were small, the size of this table, but they fired well. We did in some fifteen of them. . . . There was a loud noise here. A bomb fell on the ceiling and killed about eight of our men."

"What about you?"

"Me? What about me? I was the main person in reserve. I was in the corner when the bomb fell. . . . And then the order came."

"What order?"

"From the Committee: withdraw, Well, we see: time for a smoke. We waited a little while—and left."

"Where did you go?"

"Down to a lower floor. It was easier to fire from there." He speaks reluctantly. I wait. "Yes," he continues, after a short silence. "There was someone else here . . . likeminded . . . like a wife."

"Well?"

"Well, nothing . . . the Cossacks killed her."

The day is waning outside the window.

MARCH 13

Elena's married. She lives here in Moscow. I don't know anything else about her. In the mornings, on my days off, I wander along the boulevard around her house. The hoarfrost is like down; snow crunches under my feet. I hear the clock chime the hours slowly in the tower: it's already ten a.m. I sit on a bench, and patiently consider the hour. I tell myself: *I didn't meet her yesterday, but I will today.*

It was last year that I saw her for the first time. In the spring I was passing through the town of N.[5] In the morning I went to a large, shady park. Mighty oaks and graceful poplars stood over the damp ground. It was quiet, as in church. Even the birds weren't singing. The only sound was the burbling of a brook. I looked at its ripples. The sun gleamed on the water. I listened to the voice of the water. I raised my eyes. A woman was standing on the opposite bank behind a network of branches. She didn't notice me. But I already knew that she was hearing what I heard.

That woman was Elena.

MARCH 14

I'm in my room. Someone upstairs is playing the piano. Footsteps are lost in the soft carpet.

I've grown accustomed to this illegal life. I've grown accustomed to the loneliness. I don't wish to know the future. I try to forget about the past. I have no homeland, no name, and no family. I tell myself:

Un grand sommeil noir
Tombe sur ma vie:
Dormez, tout espoir,
Dormez, toute envie![6]

But hope doesn't die. Hope for what? For "the morning star"? I know that if we killed yesterday, we'll kill again today, too, and inevitably we'll kill tomorrow as well. "The third angel poured out

5. A Russian convention to indicate place names.

6. This quatrain and the next two come from a poem by the French decadent poet Paul Verlaine (1844–1896). "A deep dark sleep / Descends on my life: / Sleep, all hope, / Sleep, all desire!"

his vial upon the rivers and fountains of waters; and they became blood."[7] Well, you can't wash away blood with water and you can't burn it with fire. It will follow you to your grave.

Je ne vois plus rien,
Je perds la mémoire
Du mal et du bien . . .
O, la triste histoire! [8]

Happy is he who believes in the resurrection of Christ, in the resurrection of Lazarus.[9] Happy is he who also believes in socialism, in the coming paradise on earth. But I find these old tales ridiculous, and fifteen acres of apportioned land don't tempt me.[10] I said: I don't want to be a slave. Can it be that this constitutes my freedom? What pitiful freedom . . . what do I need it for? In the name of what do I commit murder? Is it in the name of terror, for the sake of the revolution? In the name of blood, for the sake of blood?

Je suis un berceau,
Qu'une main balance
Au creux d'un caveau:
Silence, silence! [11]

MARCH 17

I don't know why I'm embracing terror . . . but I know why many others are. Heinrich is convinced that it's necessary for the victo-

7. Book of Revelation 16:4.
8. "I don't see anymore, / I lose my memory / Of good and evil . . . / Oh, the sad story!"
9. See John 11.
10. A reference to an idea first expressed by the Russian anarchist Peter Kropotkin (1842–1921).
11. "I am a cradle, / Which someone's hand rocks / At the mouth of a cave: / Silence, silence!"

ry of socialism. Fyodor's wife was murdered. Erna says that she's ashamed to live. Vanya . . . but let Vanya speak for himself.

The day before he drove me around Moscow all day. I told him to meet me at Sukharevka in a sordid tavern.

He arrives wearing high boots and a light coat. He now has a beard and his hair is cut in a straight line. He says, "Listen, have you ever thought about Christ?"

"About whom?" I ask.

"About Christ? The God-man Christ? Have you ever asked what to believe and how to live? You know, when I'm home, in the courtyard, I often read the Gospel and it seems to me that there are two paths, only two. On one—everything is allowed. Do you understand? Everything. And the other—Smerdyakov.[12] If, of course, one dares, if one resolves to do everything. Since, if there's no God and Christ is a man, there's no love, and that means there's nothing . . . and the other path is the way of Christ and leads to Him. . . . Listen, since if you feel love, real genuine love, then it's possible to commit murder, isn't it?"

I say, "It's always possible to kill."

"No, not always. No, to kill is a great sin. But remember: 'Greater love hath no man than this, that a man lay down his soul for his friends.'[13] Not one's life, but one's soul. Understand this: he must accept his own torment; he must resolve to do everything out of love for the sake of love. But absolutely out of love and for the sake of love. Otherwise—it's Smerdyakov once again, that is, the path to Smerdyakov. Here I am alive. For what? Perhaps I'm living for my last hour on earth. I pray: 'O, Lord, give me death in the name of love.' One doesn't pray about committing murder. You will kill, but you don't pray. . . . And yet I know, I have little love in me, and my cross is heavy to bear.

12. The name of the half brother and servant in Dostoevsky's novel *The Brothers Karamazov* (1879–1880) who actually commits the parricide when he murders Fyodor Pavlovich.

13. John 15:13.

"Don't laugh," he says a minute later. "Why are you laughing and at what? I'm quoting God's words, and you think I'm raving. Go on, tell me, am I raving?"

I remain silent.

"You recall, John said in the Book of Revelation: 'And in those days shall men seek death, and shall not find it; and shall desire to die, and death shall flee from them.'[14] Tell me, is there anything worse than death fleeing from you when you're calling for it and seeking it? And you will seek it. We will all seek it. How dare we shed blood? How dare we break the law? Yet we do shed blood and we do break the law. You have no law; for you blood is like water. But listen to me, listen: there will come a day when you'll recall these words. You'll seek an end, but you won't find it: death will flee from you. I believe in Christ, I believe. But I'm not with Him. I'm unworthy of being with Him, because I'm covered with mud and blood. But Christ, in His mercy, will be with me."

I stare at him intently. I say, "So don't commit murder. Give up the terror."

He turns pale. "How can you say that? How dare you? Here I am going to commit murder. My soul is suffering agony. But I can't not do it, because I love. If my cross is heavy—take it. If my sin is great—receive it. But God has mercy and He will forgive.

"And forgive," he repeats in a whisper.

"Vanya, this is all rubbish. Don't think about it."

He makes no reply.

Out on the street I forget his words.

MARCH 19

Erna is whimpering. Through her tears she says, "You've completely stopped loving me."

---

14. Book of Revelation 9:6.

She's sitting in my armchair, covering her face with her hands. It's strange: never before have I noticed what large hands she has. I look closely at them and say, "Don't cry, Erna."

She raises her eyes. Her nose is red and her lower lip droops unpleasantly. I turn away to the window. She stands up and timidly touches my sleeve. "Don't be angry. I won't cry."

She cries frequently. At first her eyes redden, then her cheeks begin to swell, finally a tear rolls down her cheek imperceptibly. She cries quietly.

I take her onto my knees. "Listen, Erna, have I ever said that I love you?"

"No."

"Have I ever deceived you? Haven't I said that I love another woman?"

She shudders and makes no reply.

"Come on. Speak."

"Yes. You did say that."

"Listen to me. When I get tired of you, I won't lie, I'll tell you. Do you believe me?"

"Oh, yes."

"So now don't cry. I'm not with anyone else. I'm with you." I kiss her. Now happy, she says, "My dear, how I love you."

But I can't take my eyes off her large hands.

MARCH 21

I don't know a word of English. In the hotel, in the restaurant, on the street I speak in broken Russian. Misunderstandings occur.

Yesterday I was in the theater. Next to me sat a merchant, fat, ruddy, with a sweaty face. He was breathing heavily through his nose and dozing sullenly. During the intermission he turned to me: "What's your nationality?"

I didn't reply.

"I'm asking you, what is your nationality?"

Without looking at him I answered, "I'm a subject of His Majesty, the King of England."

He asked again: "Whose subject?"

I raised my head and replied, "I'm English."

"English? Yes, sir, yes, yes . . . the worst nation there is. Yes. They're the ones who went on the Japanese torpedo boats, sank our Russian flagship at Tsushima, captured Port Arthur.[15] . . . And now, you've come here to Russia. No, I won't allow it."

A group of curious people gathered. I said, "I ask you to keep quiet."

He continued, "Let's turn him in to the police. He may be a Japanese spy or a swindler of some sort. . . . An Englishman. I know those types, those English. . . . Why don't the police keep a lookout?"

I felt the revolver in my pocket. "For the second time: I ask you to keep quiet."

"Quiet? No, my friend, let's go the police station. They'll sort it out. We don't allow spies into the country. No. Hurrah for the tsar! God be with us!"

I got up. I looked directly into his round, bloodshot eyes and said very softly, "I'm asking you for the last time: be quiet."

He shrugged his shoulders and sat down in silence.

I left the theater.

MARCH 24

Heinrich is twenty-two years old. He's a former student. Not that long ago he was giving speeches at gatherings, wearing a pince-nez

15. The Battle of Port Arthur (1904) marked the commencement of the Russo-Japanese War. It began with a surprise night attack by a squadron of Japanese destroyers on the Russian fleet anchored at Port Arthur, Manchuria. The Battle of Tsushima (1905) was a major naval battle fought between Russia and Japan during that war. In it the Japanese fleet destroyed two-thirds of the Russian fleet. The destruction of the Russian navy caused a bitter reaction from the Russian public, which induced a peace treaty in September 1905 without any further battles.

and sporting long hair. Now, like Vanya, he's become coarse, grown thin, and goes about unshaven. His horse is also lean, its harness worn, and his sleigh is secondhand—he's a genuine Russian *muzhik*.[16]

He's driving us—Erna and me. Once we are past the town gate he turns and says, "The other day I was driving a priest. He wanted an address in Sobachya Square and offered me fifteen kopecks. Well, where is it, this Sobachya Square? I drove and drove, around and around. Finally the priest began to abuse me: 'Where are you going, you son of a bitch? I'll turn you in to the police. A driver should know the town like he knows a sack of oats; but you,' he says, 'must have bribed your way through the exam.' I had trouble placating him: 'Forgive me, father, for Christ's sake.... I really never took the exam. I gave the tramp Karpukha fifty kopecks to take the test for me.'"

Erna's hardly listening. Heinrich continues with enthusiasm: "A few days ago I was driving a lady and a gentleman. Old folks. Seemed to be nobility. I emerged onto Dolgorukovskaya Street, and there an electric streetcar was paused at a stop. Well, without even looking, Lord bless me, I drove across the rails. How that gentleman jumped up and punched me in the neck: 'Are you a scoundrel, or what? Are you trying to get us run over? Where are you rushing, you son of a bitch?' And I say, 'Don't be alarmed, your Excellency; the streetcar is paused at the stop. We'll get across.' Then I hear the woman begin to speak in French: 'Jean, don't be upset. In the first place, it's not good for you; in addition, even the driver's a human being.' So help me God, that's what she said: 'The driver's a human being.' And he answers her in Russian: 'I know that he's a human being, but what a beast he is.' She says, 'Oh, Jean, you should be ashamed to talk like that.' . . . Then he taps me on the shoulder: 'Forgive me,' he says, 'my friend,' and he gives me a twenty-kopeck tip. . . . They must have been Kadets. . . . [17] Giddy-up, old girl!"

16. A peasant.

17. Members of a liberal Russian political party (Constitutional Democrats) advocating a far-reaching change in Russian government toward a constitutional monarchy like Great Britain's.

Heinrich whips his poor old horse. Erna presses up against me imperceptibly.

"Well, and you, Erna Yakovleva, have you grown used to it here?" Heinrich speaks timidly. Erna answers reluctantly, "It's all right. Of course I've gotten used to it."

There's Petrovsky Park on the right, black interweaving of bare branches. On the left—the white tablecloth of a field. Behind us—Moscow. Churches gleam in the sun.

Heinrich falls silent. Only the sleigh creaks on the snow.

On Tverskaya Street I slip fifty kopecks into his hand. He removes his frost-covered cap and for a long time watches us go.

Erna whispers to me, "Can I come visit you this evening, dear?"

MARCH 28

The governor-general's expecting an attempt on his life. Last night he unexpectedly relocated to Neskuchnoe. We also moved there. Vanya, Fyodor, and Heinrich now follow him at Zamoskvorechye: at the Kaluzhskie Gates and on the Great Meadow. I roam about in Pyatnitska and Ordynka.

By now we know a great deal about him. He's tall, with a pale face and a trimmed mustache. He travels to the Kremlin twice a week, from three to five p.m. Otherwise, he stays at home. Sometimes he goes to the theater. He has three equipages. A pair of grey horses and two pairs of black horses. His coachman is not old, about forty or so, with a red fan-shaped beard. He has a new carriage with white headlamps. Sometimes his family travels in the carriage: his wife and children. But then the coachman is different. An old man with medals on his chest. We know his guard as well: two detectives, both Jews. They always travel on open sleighs with bay trotters. It's impossible to make a mistake, and I think we'll soon fix the day. Vanya will throw the first bomb . . .

MARCH 29

Andrei Petrovich has arrived from Petersburg. He's a member of the Committee.[18] He's spent many years in prison and in Siberia—the hard life of a persecuted revolutionary. He has sad eyes and a small pointed grey beard.

We're sitting in the Hermitage Restaurant. He says bashfully, "You know, George, the question has been raised at the Committee of postponing the terror temporarily. What do you think about that?"

"Waiter," I call out, "put *The Bells of Corneville* on the gramophone."[19]

Andrei Petrovich lowers his eyes. "You're not listening to me, but the question is very important. How can we reconcile terror with parliamentary work? Either we recognize this work and advance toward elections to the Duma,[20] or there's no constitution, in which case, of course, the terror . . . well, what do you think about this?"

"What do I think? Nothing."

"Think about it. Perhaps the time will come to dismiss you; that is, to disband the organization."

"What?" I ask him.

"That is, not disband it, but—how shall I put it? You know, George, after all, we understand. We know how difficult it will be for our comrades. We value them. . . . Besides, this is only a plan."

His face is the color of a lemon, and he has wrinkles around his eyes. He probably lives in a poor little room, somewhere on Vyborgskaya, makes his own tea over a spirit lamp, runs around

18. Presumably, the central body of the terrorist organization.

19. *Les cloches de Corneville* (1876; known in English as *The Chimes of Normandy* or *The Bells of Corneville*) is a comic operetta in three acts by Robert Planquette (1848–1903), probably the most popular French operetta of all time.

20. Russian assembly with advisory or legislative functions. The first formally constituted one was the State Duma introduced into the Russian Empire by Tsar Nicholas II in 1906.

during the winter in his fall coat, and is up to his neck in all sorts of plans and matters. He's making a revolution.

I say, "Listen here, Andrei Petrovich, you decide as you like. It's your right. But however you decide, the governor-general will be killed."

"What are you saying? You won't submit to the Committee?"

"No."

"Listen, George—"

"I've spoken, Andrei Petrovich."

"And the Party?" he reminds me.

"And the terror?" I answer him.

He sighs. Then he extends his hand to me. "I won't say anything in Petersburg. Maybe things will turn out all right somehow. Don't be angry."

"I'm not angry."

"Goodbye, George."

"Goodbye, Andrei Petrovich."

The stars were out. A sign of the coming frost. It felt uncanny in the empty side streets. Andrei Petrovich hastened to the station. The poor old man, the poor grown-up child. Yet theirs is the kingdom of heaven.

MARCH 30

Once again I am wandering near Elena's house. It's a huge, grey, massive building belonging to the merchant Kuporosov. How can people live in a box like that? How can Elena live here?

I know: it's foolish to freeze out on the street, to circle around these locked doors, and to wait for something that will never happen. Well, and even if I were to meet her? What would change? Nothing.

But just yesterday I met Elena's husband at Datsiaro's shop on Kuznetskaya Street. I noticed him from a distance. He stood at the window, his back to me, and was looking at some photographs. I went up and stood right next to him. He's a tall man, blond and well built. He's about twenty-five. An officer. He turned around and recognized me at once. I could see the malice and jealousy in his darkened eyes. I don't know what he saw in mine.

I'm not jealous of him. I harbor no malice toward him. But he bothers me. He's standing in my way. Furthermore, when I think about him, I recall the words:

> If a louse in your shirt
> Shouts that you're a flea—Go out to the street
> And kill![21]

APRIL 2

There's a thaw today; streams are running. Puddles gleam in the sun. Snow is melting and in Sokolniki Park it smells of spring—of the strong damp of the forest. There's still frost at night, but in the afternoon the road is slippery and the roofs are beginning to drip.

Last spring I was in the south. The nights were pitch black; only the constellation Orion was clearly visible. In the morning I would walk along the gravel beach to the sea. Heather was blooming in the woods, as well as white lilies. I made my way up onto the cliff. The scorching sun shone above me, and below—the transparent green of the water. Lizards darted along; the cicadas were buzzing. I lay on the hot stones and listened to the sound of the waves. And suddenly—everything would vanish, no me, no sea, no sun, no forest, no spring flowers. There was only one vast body, one eternal and blessed life.

But now?

One of my acquaintances, a Belgian officer, told me about his service in the Congo. He was alone and had fifty black soldiers. His cordon was located on the bank of a large river, in virgin forest, where the sun didn't shine and where yellow fever was prevalent. On the other side of the river lived a tribe of independent Negroes

21. Source unknown.

with their own king and their own laws. Night followed day and then a new day dawned. In the morning, and the afternoon, and the evening the same murky river flowed by with its sandy banks, the same bright green woody vines, the same people with black skin and incomprehensible language. Sometimes from boredom he would take his rifle and try to hit a curly head amid the branches. And when the black people on this side of the river happened to catch someone who lived on the other side, they would tie the captive to a post. Because they had nothing to do they would shoot at him for target practice. And vice versa: when one of his people turned up on the other bank, they would cut off his arms and legs. Then they would place him in the river at night with only his head sticking out. In the morning they would cut off his head.

I ask: how is the white man different from black men? What distinguishes us from them? It's one of two things: either "Thou shalt not kill," and then we're the same kind of rogues as Pobedonostev and Trepov.[22] And if it's "An eye for an eye and a tooth for a tooth," then what need is there for justification? I want to do something and I do it. Does this perhaps hide some cowardice, fear of someone's opinion? Fear that others will say "murderer" when now they're saying "hero"? But what do I care about other people's opinions?

Raskolnikov killed the old woman and he himself was choked by her blood.[23] Yet Vanya goes out to kill, and will feel happy and holy. He says, "In the name of love." But does love really exist on earth? Did Christ really rise from the dead on the third day? It's all words. . . . No—

22. Konstantin Petrovich Pobedonostsev (1827–1907) was a Russian jurist, statesman, and adviser to three tsars. He was the chief spokesman for reactionary positions. Alexander Fyodorovitch Trepov (1862–1928) was the prime minister of the Russian Empire from November 23, 1916, until January 9, 1917. He was a conservative, a monarchist, a member of the Russian Assembly, and an advocate of moderate and sane reforms.

23. The hero of Dostoevsky's classic novel *Crime and Punishment* (1866).

If a louse in your shirt
Shouts that you're a flea—Go out to the street
And kill!

APRIL 4

Fyodor relates an incident: "This happened in the south in the town of N. You know the street that runs down from the station? Where a guard stands on a hill? I took a bomb—one that I made myself—and wrapped it in a scarf, and climbed up. I stand not far from the guard, maybe twenty-five paces away. And I wait. I watch and see a cloud of dust: the Cossacks are coming. And behind them, the man himself, in a carriage with some officer sitting next to him. I raise my arm and hold the bomb up high. He glances over and sees me, white as a sheet. I look at him and he looks at me. Then I, God bless me, I throw the bomb down with a wide swing. I hear: it exploded. Well, I take off running. I had a Browning revolver, a good one, a gift from Vanya. I turn around: the guard aims his rifle at me. I begin to spin around, to make it hard for him. I turn and fire from my revolver. The main thing was to frighten him. I fire all my bullets, change the cartridge, and run farther. I look: soldiers come running out of the barracks, infantry. They fire at me with their rifles on the run. They should have stopped so that they could have shot from one place. They would have killed me on the spot. Well, I run across the field, and run up to the houses. What's this? Sailors come running from the lane. Well, I go bang-bang-bang and use up the whole cartridge clip again. I don't know whether I killed anyone. I keep running. I turn into a street—factory men are coming from work. I join them. I hear: 'Don't touch him, lads, let him run.' I hide in the crowd, put the revolver in my pocket, take off my hat, put on a cap, throw off my jacket, and remain in my shirt. . . . I light up a cigarette, and merge with the others. I keep on. As if I, too, came from the factory, heading to meet the soldiers."

"Well?"

"Well, nothing. I came home. At home I hear: the bomb blew up the carriage, blew his innards to pieces, and killed two Cossacks."

"Tell me," I ask, "if we kill the governor-general, will you be content?"

"If we kill the gentleman?"

"Well, yes."

He smiles. His strong teeth, white as milk, sparkle. "You strange man . . . of course I'll be content."

"But, Fyodor, they'll hang you."

He says, "So what? Two minutes—and it's all over. We'll all end up there."

"Where?"

He laughs loudly. "With the damn pigs."

APRIL 6

Holy Week has ended.[24] Today the joyful bells are ringing: it's Easter. Last night there was a festive religious procession, in praise of Christ. And this morning the streets are filled with strollers; there's no room for an apple to fall. Peasant women with white kerchiefs, soldiers, tramps, and high school students. They exchange kisses, crack sunflower seeds, and make jokes. Hawkers' stands sell eggs dyed red, spice cookies, American devils,[25] and colored balloons tied onto ribbons. People are like bees in a hive. Hubbub and noise.

In my childhood you would prepare for Communion during the sixth week of Lent. Fast all week, and not a morsel of food on the day of the sacrament. During the last week before Easter you would genuflect endlessly, clinging to Christ's shroud in church: "Lord, forgive me my sins." At Easter matins, it was as if we were in paradise: candles were brightly lit, the odor of wax, white garments,

24. The week before Easter Sunday.

25. A popular child's toy consisting of a puppet dipped in a bottle of water, which when pulled up and down could be made to perform.

the golden icon-case. You'd stand and hardly breathe—*will we go home soon with the holy Easter cake?* At home it was a holiday, a great celebration. All of Holy Week was a holiday.

But today everything seems alien to me. The church bell is annoying; the laughter is boring. I'd like to go away anywhere and never come back.

"Sir, try your luck," a little girls says to me and slips me an envelope.

The girl is barefoot, ragged, and not very cheerful. On a piece of grey paper my fortune is written:

If failure pursues you, don't lose hope and don't yield to despair. You will overcome the most difficult things and will turn the wheel of fortune in your favor. Your enterprise will end in complete success that you dare not even expect.

Isn't this a nice Easter egg for the holiday?

APRIL 7

Vanya lives on Miusy in the hostelry of a workers' cooperative. He sleeps side by side with other men on benches. He eats out of a common pot. He grooms his horse himself and cleans his carriage. During the day he's at work outside. He doesn't complain; he's content.

Today he's wearing a new coat; his hair is oiled and his boots creak. He says, "Easter's come. Good . . . Christ has risen, George."

"Well, so what if He's risen?"

"Oh, you . . . there's no joy in you. You won't accept the world."

"Do you?"

"Me? Me—that's another matter. I feel sorry for you, George."

"Sorry?"

"Well, yes. You don't love anyone. Even yourself. You know, we have a driver in the courtyard, Tikhon. He's such a dark-skinned, curly-haired peasant. He's mean as the devil. At one time he was rich, then he lost everything in a fire: they burned him out. He still can't forgive the act. He curses everyone: God, the tsar, students, merchants, even children. He hates even them. 'They're all sons of bitches,' he says, 'all scoundrels. They suck the blood of Christians and God rejoices in the heavens. . . . ' The other day I came into the courtyard after having tea and I saw: Tikhon was standing in the middle of the yard. His feet were spread wide, his sleeves rolled up; he has enormous fists—and he was lashing his horse across the eyes with his reins. The poor horse was decrepit, hardly breathing, jerking her head to avoid the blows. But he kept lashing her across the eyes, the eyes. 'You wretch,' he shouted hoarsely, 'you damned swine. I'll show you, I'll teach you . . . '

"'Why are you beating the poor beast, Tikhon?' I say. 'Shut up,' he cries, 'you rotten jerk!' And he begins lashing her even more ferociously. There's mud in the courtyard, stench, horse manure, and all the other drivers came out and stood there laughing: 'Tikhon's having fun,' they said. Just like you, George, would like to lash everyone across the eyes . . . oh, you poor thing."[26]

He bites off a small piece of sugar, lingers over his tea, and then he says, "Don't be angry. And don't laugh. I'm thinking. Do you know what about? We are poor in spirit. What do we live by, my friend? We live by bare hatred. We don't know how to love. We strangle, we stab, we burn. And we are strangled, hanged, and burned. In the name of what? Tell me. No, tell me."

I shrug my shoulders. "Vanya, ask Heinrich."

"Heinrich? He believes in socialism; he knows that people will be free and satiated. But that's all for Martha; what about Mary?[27] One may give one's life for freedom, of course. Not only for freedom. One may give one's life for one tear. I pray: let there be no more slaves and let there be no more hungry people. But that's not everything, George. We know that the world lives by untruths. Where is there truth, tell me?"

"What is the Truth? Is that what you mean?"

26. This recalls Raskolnikov's horrendous dream of the beaten mare in part one of Dostoevsky's *Crime and Punishment.*

27. Luke 10:38–42.

"Yes, what is the Truth? Do you recall: 'To this end was I born, and for this cause came I into the world, that I should bear witness unto the truth. Every one that is of the truth heareth my voice.'"[28]

"Vanya, Christ said: 'Thou shalt not kill.'"

"I know. But for now don't talk about blood. Say something else: Europe has uttered two great words to the world and has sealed these two things with its suffering. The first word is freedom; the second is socialism. Well, and what have we Russians had to tell the world? Blood has been spilled for freedom. Who believes in it now? Has blood been shed for socialism? What, in your opinion, is socialism? Paradise on earth? Well, and for love, in the name of love, has anyone gone to the stake? Has anyone of us dared to say: it's not enough that people were free; it's not enough that children weren't dying of hunger, so that mothers weren't dissolving in tears. It's still necessary for people to love one another, for God to be with them and in them. We've forgotten about God and about love. But one half of the truth is in Martha; the other half is in Mary. Where is our Mary? Listen, I believe: in the cause of the peasants, of Christians, of Christ. In God's name, in the name of love. And people will be free and satiated, and they will live in love. I believe: our people, God's people, people of love, people of Christ. Our word is of resurrection: 'Lord, come out!' We are lacking in faith and we are weak as children; therefore we wield the sword. We raise it not because we are strong but out of fear and weakness. Wait, tomorrow others will come, they will be pure. They won't need the sword because they'll be strong. But we'll perish before they come. Our children's grandchildren will love God, live in God, rejoice over Christ. The world will open up to them anew, and they will behold in it what we don't see. And as for today, George, Christ is risen, it's holy Easter. Well, let us forget insults on such a day, let us stop lashing across the eyes . . ."

He's silently thoughtful.

"What, Vanya? What are you thinking about?"

28. John 18:37.

"Just this, listen: the chain is unbroken. There's no exit for me, no way out. I go forward to kill, but I believe in the Word, I worship Christ. I feel the pain, the agony . . ."

The tavern is full of drunken noise. People are celebrating the holiday. Vanya leans over the tablecloth and waits. What can I do to him? Lash him with reins across his eyes?

APRIL 8

I'm with Vanya again. He says, "Do you know when I came to know Christ? When I saw God for the first time? I was in Siberia, in exile. Once I went on a hunt. It was in the estuary of the Ob River. Where the Ob flows into the ocean it's like a sea. The sky is low and grey; the river is also grey, as are the crests of the waves; you can't see the banks of the river, as if they didn't exist at all. A boat landed me on a small island. We agreed: they would come to collect me in the evening. Well, I roamed the island, shooting ducks. There was a swamp, rotting birch trees, green mounds, and moss. I walked and walked, straying away from the edge of the island. I shot one duck; it fell but I couldn't find it. I looked among the mounds. Meanwhile it was evening; a fog arose from the river and it became dark. I decided to make my way back to the riverbank. I used the direction of the wind to find my path, and walked. I started out. I felt that my feet were sinking. I wanted to climb up on a mound—but no, I was sinking in the swampy quagmire. You know, I was drowning slowly, a rate of about half an inch every minute. A cold north wind began to blow and it started to rain. I pulled one foot, but it didn't come out and it became worse: it sank in another inch. I raised my gun and began firing into the air out of desperation. Perhaps they'd hear it and come to help me. No, only silence; I could only hear the wind whistling. So there I stood, almost up to my knees in the muck. I thought: I'll sink into the swamp, bubbles will rise to the surface over me, and just as before there will be only green mounds. I felt disgusted, to the point of tears. I pulled my leg once again—but it was still worse. I felt cold as ice and was shivering like an aspen: what an end, at the edge of the world, to die like a fly . . . and you know, my heart suddenly felt empty. It didn't matter—nothing mattered; I would perish. I bit my lips until they bled, and with my last strength tried to pull out my leg. I managed to pull my foot free. All of a sudden I felt happy. I looked; my boot was stuck in the swamp, and my foot was bleeding. Somehow I managed to place one foot on a mound, leaned on my gun, and drew out the other foot. Well, I stood there on my own two feet and was afraid to budge. I thought: if I take a step, I'll wind up back in the quagmire. So I stood there all night in one spot until dawn; rain was falling, the sky was dark, the wind was howling, and on that very night I understood, you know, with all my heart, I understood completely: God is above us and with us. And I was not afraid, but joyful, and a great weight fell from my heart. In the morning my comrades arrived and rescued me."

"Many people see God just before death. It's a result of fear, Vanya."

"Fear? Well, perhaps. Only what do you think? That God can appear to you here in this filthy tavern? Before death the soul becomes tense, when the end is in sight. That's why people see God more often than ever before death. I've seen Him, too.

"Listen to this," he continues, after a pause. "It's a great joy to see God. While you don't know Him, you don't think about Him at all. You think about everything else, but not about Him. Some people dream about the superman.[29] Just think: the superman. And they believe that they have found the philosopher's stone, the secret to life.[30] In my opinion, that's like Smerdyakov. They say, 'I can't love those close to me, on the other hand, I love those farthest from

29. The concept of the Übermensch was formulated by Friedrich Nietzsche (1844–1900) and expressed in *Thus Spoke Zarathrustra* (1883).

30. The philosopher's stone is a legendary alchemical substance capable of turning base metals such as mercury into gold or silver. It was also thought to extend one's life and was called the elixir of life, useful both for rejuvenation and for achieving immortality.

me.' How can you love those farthest away, if there's no love in you for those near you? You know, it's easy to die for others, to give people your death. But it's harder to give people your life. From day to day, minute to minute, to live in love, God's love for people, for all living creatures. To forget about oneself, to arrange life not for oneself, not for some remote people. We've become cruel, turned into wild beasts. Hey, dear friend, it's bitter to watch: people rush about, search, believe in Chinese gods, in wooden logs, but they can't believe in God, and don't want to love Christ. Poison burns in us from our childhood. Take Heinrich: he won't ever say 'flower'; he says, 'flower of a certain family, such and such species, with certain petals and a certain corolla.' As a result of this rubbish, he doesn't see the flower. In the same way we don't see God because of the rubbish. It's all mathematics and reason. And out there, when I stood in the rain on the mound in the swamp, waiting for my death, there I understood: in addition to reason there's still something else; we have blinds on our eyes and we don't see, we don't know. Why are you laughing, George?"

"You sound just like a parish priest."

"Well, so be it. But you tell me—can one live without love?"

"Of course one can."

"How? Tell me."

"You spit at the whole world."

"Are you joking, George?"

"No, I'm not joking."

"Poor little George, poor fellow . . ."

I say goodbye to him. I forget his words once more.

APRIL 10

I saw the governor-general today. He's a tall, handsome elderly man, who wears glasses and has a closely clipped mustache. Glancing at his serene face, no one could say that he has thousands of victims on his conscience.

I walked through the Kremlin. On the square, which yesterday was white with snow, today the paving stones were wet. The ice has melted and the Moscow River gleamed brightly in the sun. Zamoskvorechye drowned in the factory smoke. Sparrows were twittering.

There was a carriage near the palace entrance. I recognized it at once: black horses and the gold spokes of the wheels. I crossed the square and approached the palace. Just then the door swung wide open and the policeman on guard saluted. The governor-general made his way slowly down the staircase. I stood rooted to the pavement. Without tearing my eyes away, I looked at him. He raised his head and glanced at me. I doffed my hat. I lowered it before him. He smiled and raised his hand to his military cap. He bowed to me.

At that moment I hated him.

I made my way toward the Alexander Garden. My feet kept sticking in the soft clay of the paths. The jackdaws flew noisily through the birch trees. I was almost crying. I felt sorry that he was still alive.

APRIL 12

During my free time I visit the Rumyantsev Library. Female students with closely cropped hair and bearded male students sit in the quiet reading room. With my clean-shaven face and my high collar I look very different from them.

I read the ancient classics attentively. They had no conscience and were not seeking the truth. They simply lived their lives. The way grass grows and birds sing. Perhaps in this holy simplicity lies the key to the acceptance of the world.

Athena tells Odysseus:

> Surely I'll stand beside you, not forget you,
> not when the day arrives for us to do our work.

> Those men who court your wife and waste your goods?
> I have a feeling some will splatter your ample floors
> with all their blood and brains.[31]

What God can I pray to so that he doesn't desert me? Where is my defense and who is my protector? I'm alone. And if I have no defense, then I am my own protector. And since I have no God, I will be my own god. Vanya says, "If everything is permitted—that's Smerdyakov." How is Smerdyakov worse than the others? And why should I feel afraid of Smerdyakov?

> I have a feeling some will splatter your ample floors
> with all their blood and brains.

Let it be splattered. I have nothing against that.

APRIL 13

Erna says to me, "It seems to me that I've lived only to meet you. I saw you in my dreams. I prayed for you."

"Erna, what about the revolution?"

"We'll die together. . . . Listen, my dear, when I'm with you—I feel like a little girl, still a child. I know: I can't give you anything. But I have love. Take it." And she weeps.

"Erna, don't cry."

"I'm weeping for joy. . . . See, I'm no longer crying. You know, I wanted to tell you . . . Heinrich . . ."

"What about Heinrich?"

"Don't be angry. . . . Yesterday Heinrich said that he loved me."

"Well?"

"Well, I don't love him. I love only you. You're not jealous, are you, dear?" she whispers into my ear.

---

31. Homer, *The Odyssey*, trans. Robert Fagles (London: Penguin, 2006), book 13, lines 449–53.

"Jealous? Me?"

"Don't be jealous. I don't love him at all. But he's so unhappy, and I felt such pain when he said it. . . . Furthermore, it seemed to me that I shouldn't be listening to him; that I was betraying you."

"Betraying me, Erna?"

"I love you so much, my dear, and I felt so sorry for him. I told him that I was his friend. You're not angry, are you?"

"Rest assured, Erna. I'm not angry and not jealous."

She is hurt and drops her eyes. "Don't you care? Tell me, do you care at all?"

"Listen," I tell her, "some women are faithful wives, passionate lovers, and good friends. But all of them together aren't worth one kind: royal queens. She doesn't give her heart away. She grants love."

Erna listens in fear. Then she says, "Then you don't love me at all?"

I reply by kissing her. She buries her face in my chest and whispers, "But we'll die together? Right?"

"Perhaps."

She falls asleep in my arms.

APRIL 15

I go for a ride in Heinrich's carriage. Past the Arch of Triumph I say to him, "Well then, how are things?"

"It's not easy"—he shakes his head—"driving a carriage all day in the rain."

I say, "It's not easy when a man's in love."

"How do you know?" he asks, turning to me swiftly.

"Know what? I don't know anything. And I don't want to know."

"Don't make fun, George."

"I'm not making fun."

Here's the park. Gleaming drops are falling on us from the wet branches; in places there are patches of young green grass.

"George."

"Yes?"

"George, is there the possibility of an explosion during the making of a bomb?"

"It can happen."

"That means Erna might be blown up?"

"Perhaps."

"George."

"Well?"

"Why do you entrust this work to her?"

"It's her area of expertise."

"Her expertise?"

"Yes."

"Can't anyone else do it?"

"No. . . . Why are you so upset?"

"No. . . . I just . . . it's nothing. . . . I just happened to think of it." He turns back to Moscow. Halfway home he turns to me again. "George?"

"Well?"

"Will it be soon?"

"I think so."

"How soon?"

"Two weeks, maybe three."

"And it's not possible to find a replacement for Erna?"

"No."

He shrinks into his blue coat, but says nothing.

"Goodbye, Heinrich. Keep your spirits up."

"I will."

"And don't think about any one person."

"I know. You don't have to tell me. Goodbye."

He drives off slowly. This time I watch him go for a long time.

APRIL 16

I ask myself: do I really still love Elena? Or do I love only the shadow—my former love for her? Perhaps Vanya's right that I don't love anyone, and I can't, and don't know how to love. Maybe it's not worth loving.

Heinrich loves Erna and will love only her, all his life. But for him love is not a source of joy, but a source of torment. And my love—is it joy?

I'm in my room once again, in my boring room of my boring hotel. Hundreds of people live under one roof with me. I'm a stranger to them. I'm a stranger in this stone city, perhaps in the whole world. Erna gives herself to me, her whole self without thinking. But I don't want her and respond—with what? Friendship? Isn't it all pretense? It's foolish to think about Elena, and foolish to kiss Erna. But I think of the former and kiss the latter. But after all, what difference does it make?

APRIL 18

The governor-general has moved back from Neskuchnoe into his Kremlin palace. Our plans are ruined once more. We have to begin our observation all over again. It's more difficult in the Kremlin. The palace is constantly guarded by sentries; there are detectives on the square and at the gates. Every passerby comes under surveillance. Every driver is suspected.

Of course, the police don't know where we are and who we are. But rumors already circulate in Moscow. They'll hang us, but others will come after us. In any case, the governor-general will be killed.

Yesterday in the tavern I overheard the following conversation. Two men were talking; one seemed to be a sales clerk and the other must have been his assistant, a lad of about eighteen. "It's the will of God in everything," the sales clerk said insistently. "That means a bullet to one person, and a bomb to another. Listen, a young lady came to see him with a petition. They admitted her. He began reading her petition. While he read she pulled out a revolver and shot him. She planted four bullets in him."

The young lad threw up his hands. "My, my . . . well, did he die?"

"What? Nothing of the sort! They're hard to kill these days."

"Well?"

"They hanged her, of course. After a while another young lady arrived. Also with a petition."

"And did they really admit her, too?"

"No. She said this, that, and other thing. But they searched her in the entrance hall. They looked and found a revolver hidden in her braid. In other words, God saved him."

"And then?"

"They hanged her, too, of course. But what do you think?" the narrator asked, spreading his arms in surprise. "After a while he was strolling along a path in the garden. There was a guard with him. All of a sudden, a shot was fired from somewhere or other. The bullet went right through his heart. He hardly had time to scream. What came to light subsequently? A soldier shot him from the bushes. One of his own soldiers, from the guard."

"What scum they are . . . just think."

"Yes. . . . The soldier was hanged, of course, but the official died anyway. It must have been his time. Fate." He leaned low across the table and whispered, "Our Senka, you know, will be done in by a bomb. Every day there's a proclamation on the table: 'Wait,' it says, 'there's a bomb for you; soon we'll blow you up.' And remember my words: none other than they'll blow him up. Yes."

I think the same thing.

APRIL 20

Yesterday I met Elena at last. I wasn't thinking about her; I almost forgot that she was here in Moscow. I was walking along Petrovka and suddenly heard someone call. I turned around. Elena was standing in front of me. I saw her huge grey eyes, locks of her black hair. I walked alongside her. She said with a smile, "You've forgotten me."

A shaft of bright evening light shone into our faces. The street dissolved in its rays and the pavement gleamed like gold. I blushed like a poppy. I said, "No. I haven't forgotten you."

She took my arm and said softly, "Are you here for a long time?"

"I don't know."

"What are you doing here?"

"I don't know."

"You don't know?"

"No."

She blushed a deep red color. "Well, I know. I'll tell you."

"Tell me."

"You're hunting, right?"

"Perhaps."

"They'll probably hang you."

"Perhaps."

The evening rays had vanished. It was cool and grey in the street.

I wanted to tell her a great deal. But I had forgotten all my words. I said only, "Why are you here in Moscow?"

"My husband is in the service."

"Your husband?"

Suddenly I remembered about her husband. I had met him. Yes, of course, she has a husband.

"Farewell," I said, extending my hand clumsily.

"Are you in a hurry?"

"Yes, I am."

"Don't go."

I looked in her eyes. They sparkled with love. But once again I remembered: there's a husband.

"Goodbye."

It's cold and dark at night in Moscow. I came to Tivoli. The orchestra is playing and women are laughing shamelessly. I'm alone.

APRIL 25

Petersburg

The governor-general left for Petersburg. I followed him: it may be easier to kill him there. I was happy to see the Neva River and the gleaming cupolas of Saint Isaac's Cathedral. Spring is lovely in Petersburg. It's as virginal and pure as a sixteen-year-old girl.

The governor-general is heading to Peterhof to see the tsar.[32] I go on the same train, in a first-class car. A well-dressed lady enters my compartment. She drops her handkerchief. I pick it up and hand it to her. "Are you going to Peterhof?" she asks in French.

"Yes, I am."

"You're not Russian, are you?" she asks, scrutinizing me.

"I'm English."

"English? What's your name? I know you."

I hesitate a minute. Then I take out my visiting card: "George O'Brien, Engineer, London-Moscow."

"An engineer . . . I'm delighted. . . . Do call on me. I'll be waiting for you."

In Peterhof I meet her again: at the buffet in the station she's having tea with some Jew. He looks very much like a spy. I approach her. I say, "Pleased to meet you again." She laughs.

We walk along the platform. The platform is divided into two parts by rows of gendarmes. I ask, "Why are there so many gendarmes here?"

"You don't know? An attempt on the life of the governor-general of Moscow is being planned. He's in Peterhof now, traveling on this train. Oh, those good-for-nothing anarchists . . ."

"An attempt on the life . . . of the governor-general?"

"Ha ha ha. . . . He doesn't know. . . . Don't act out a comedy."

In the train car the conductor comes to take our tickets. She hands him a grey envelope. I read the printed words PETERSBURG DEPARTMENT OF GENDARMES.[33]

"You probably have a season ticket?" I ask her.

---

32. An imperial palace complex built by Peter the Great in the early eighteenth century in the environs of Petersburg.

33. The Special Corps of Gendarmes was the uniformed security police of the Russian Empire in the nineteenth and early twentieth centuries. Its main responsibilities were law enforcement and state security.

She blushes deeply. "No, it's just that . . . it's nothing . . . a gift. Ah, I'm so pleased to make your acquaintance. . . . I so like the English."

The train whistles. Petersburg station. I bid farewell to her and follow her stealthily. She enters the gendarmerie.

"A spy," I say to myself.

In the hotel I think: either I'm being followed, and in that case, of course, all is lost, or this meeting was an accident, a boring coincidence. I want to know the whole truth. I want to test fate.

I put on my top hat. I take a smart cab. I ring at the entrance to the address. "Is the lady at home?"

"Come in."

The room is like a *bonbonière*.[34] In the corner there's a bouquet of tea roses: a floral tribute. Portraits of the lady of the house in a variety of poses adorn the tables and walls.

"Ah, you've come. How very nice. Have a seat."

We speak French again. I smoke a cigar and hold my top hat on my lap.

"Do you live in Moscow?"

"Yes, I do."

"Do you like Russian ladies?"

"They're the best in the world."

There's a knock at the door.

"Come in."

Two gentlemen enter, with very dark hair and large mustaches. They are either cardsharps or pimps. We shake hands.

All three of them move over to the window.

"Who's that?" I hear them whisper.

"That? Ah, an English engineer, very rich. You can talk, don't mind him: he doesn't speak a word of Russian."

I stand up. "I'm sorry, but I must go. Goodbye."

We shake hands again. Out on the street I laugh: thank heavens that I'm English.

34. A small fancy box or dish for bonbons.

APRIL 26

Petersburg

The governor-general is on his way back to Moscow. I wander around Petersburg without any goal.

It's getting dark. The twilight over the Neva is purple. The clear-cut spire of the Fortress pierces the sky.[35]

There's a tricolored sentry box at the oak gates of the prison, the symbol of our slavery. Behind the white wall stands a dark, gaping corridor. The echo of footsteps on the stone slabs. Darkness, bars on the windows. At night the trembling sound of the clock chimes. Great sadness upon the entire earth.

Many of my friends have been hanged here. Many more will be hanged.

I see the low bastions, the grey walls. We have too little strength to take revenge, too little to beat stone upon stone. But the day of great wrath will come . . .

Who will withstand it on that day?

APRIL 28

It's still chilly in the park. The linden trees are bare, but the hazelnut trees have already leafed out. Birds are singing in the green bushes.

Elena leans down and picks some flowers. She turns to me and laughs, "How nice it is. . . . Isn't it true that it's bright and cheerful today?"

Yes, I feel bright and cheerful. I look her in the eye and feel like telling her that she's the bright light and joy of the day. I join in her laughter involuntarily.

35. The Peter and Paul Fortress is the original citadel of Petersburg, founded by Peter the Great in 1703 and built to Domenico Trezzini's designs from 1706 to 1740.

"It's been so long since I've seen you. . . . Where have you been? Where have you been living? What have you seen? What have you learned? What have you been thinking about me?" And, not expecting an answer, she blushes. "I felt so afraid for you."

I don't recall a morning like this. The lilies of the valley are in bloom; there is a fragrance of spring. Fluffy clouds melt in the sky as they chase one another. I feel joy once again in my soul: she felt afraid for me.

"You know, I live and don't even notice life. I look at you and it seems that you're not really you, but someone else, but still very nice. Yes, after all, you're a stranger to me. . . . Do I really know you? Do you know me? And it's unnecessary. . . . We don't have to know anything. We're happy like this, aren't we? Isn't it true?"

After a pause, she says with a smile, "No, tell me, what have you been doing? How have you been living?"

"But you know how I've been living."

She drops her eyes. "Then it's true? The terror?"

"Yes."

A shadow crosses her face. She takes me by the hand and stays silent. "Listen," she says at last. "I don't understand anything about it . . . but tell me, why kill? Why? Just look at how nice it is here: spring is in bloom; birds are singing. And you're thinking of what? Living by what? Death? Why is that, sweetheart?"

I want to tell her that blood purifies blood, that we kill against our desire, that terror is necessary for the revolution, and that revolution is necessary for the people. But for some reason I can't say these words to her. I know that all this would be only words to her and that she wouldn't understand me.

But she repeats insistently, "Why, sweetheart?"

There's dew on the trees. If you brush a branch with your shoulder—a shower of glistening drops descends. I keep silent.

"Isn't it better to live, simply to live? Or else I don't understand you. Or else, it's necessary to do that. . . . No, no," she answers herself, "it's not necessary, it can't be necessary."

I ask timidly, like a boy, "What is necessary, Elena?"

"You're asking me? You? As if I know? Can I really know? I don't know a thing . . . and I don't want to know. . . . But we're happy today . . . and we shouldn't think about death. . . . We shouldn't . . ."

Once again she picks some flowers with a laugh, and I think—soon I'll be alone again, and her girlish laughter will sound not for me, but for another. Blood rushes to my face. I say barely audibly, "Elena."

"What, my dear?"

"You ask me what I've been doing. I've been thinking about you."

"Thinking about me?"

"Yes. . . . Don't you see: I love you."

She drops her eyes. "Don't say that to me."

"Why not?"

"My God . . . don't say it. Goodbye." She leaves quickly. Her black dress is visible from time to time among the white birches for a long while.

APRIL 29

I wrote a letter to Elena:

It seems as if I haven't seen you for several years. Every hour and every minute I feel that you are not with me. Day and night, always and everywhere—I see your shining eyes.

I believe in love, in my right to love. In the depths of my heart, at the very bottom of it, there resides serene certainty, a premonition of the future. It must come to pass. It will be so.

I love you and I'm happy. May you also be happy in this love.

I received a brief reply:

Tomorrow in Sokolniki Park, at six o'clock.

APRIL 30

Elena says to me, "I'm glad, happy that you're with me . . . but don't talk to me about love."

I keep silent.

"No, promise me: don't talk about love. . . . And don't be sad; don't think about anything."

"I was thinking about you."

"Me? Don't think about me."

"Why not?" And I myself reply immediately, "You're married? Your husband? Your husband's honor? The duty of a married woman? Oh, forgive me, of course . . . I dared to speak about my love; I dared to ask for yours. For virtuous wives there's only domestic serenity, the pure chambers of the heart. Forgive me."

"Aren't you ashamed of yourself?"

"No, I'm not ashamed. I know: the tragedy of love, of the wedding gown, of a legal marriage, of legal conjugal kisses. It isn't me who's ashamed, Elena, but you?"

"Be quiet."

For several minutes we walk in silence along a narrow path in the park. Anger still shows in her face. "Listen," she says, turning to me. "Is it possible that you recognize any law?"

"I don't, but you do."

"No . . . but surely . . . you live by blood. Let's say it's necessary, but you . . . why do you live by blood?"

"I don't know."

"You don't?"

"No."

"Listen, but, it's the law. . . . You said to yourself, 'It's necessary.'"

After a pause, I say, "No. I said, 'I want to.'"

"So you want to?" She looks straight into my eyes with astonishment.

"Well, so you want to?"

"Yes." Suddenly she gently places her hands on my shoulders. "My dear, sweet George."

And with a swift, graceful movement she kisses me right on the lips. Long and passionately. I open my eyes: she's no longer there. Where is she? Was this perhaps a dream I had?

MAY 1

Today's the first of May—a workers' holiday. I love this day. It has so much light and joy. But precisely today, I would gladly kill the governor-general.

He's become cautious. He hides in his palace and we follow him in vain. We see only his detectives and soldiers. And they see us. Therefore I think that we'll have to terminate our surveillance.

I learned: on the fourteenth, Coronation Day, he will visit the theater. We'll post guards at the Kremlin Gates. Vanya will stand at Spassky Gate, Fyodor at Trinity, and Heinrich at Borovichi. And we'll patiently await him.

I rejoice in advance of our victory. I see blood on his uniform. I see the dark vaults of the church lit with candles. I hear the chanting of prayers and smell the incense. I wish his death.

I wish him "fire and a lake of fire."[36]

MAY 2

These days it's as if I have a fever. My entire will is concentrated in one thing: in my desire to kill. Each day I look carefully: am I being followed by spies? I'm afraid that we will sow, but won't get to reap, and that we'll be arrested. But I won't give up alive.

I'm now living at the Bristol Hotel. Yesterday they brought me my passport. A detective came from the police station. He lingers on the threshold and says, "May I ask—the police inspector wants to know—to which religion do you belong?"

A strange question. In my passport it says that I'm Lutheran. Without turning my head I say, "What?"

"What religion are you? What faith?"

I take my passport in hand. I read aloud the English title of Lord Lansdowne: "We, Henry Charles Keith Petty-Fitzmaurice, Mar-

36. Book of Revelation 20:14, "And death and hell were cast into the lake of fire."

quess of Lansdowne, Earl Wycombe," etc. I can't read English. I pronounce each letter separately. The detective listens attentively. "Do you understand?"

"Yes, sir."

I say with a strong accent, "Go back to the office and tell them: I will send a telegram at once to the ambassador. Do you understand?"

"Yes, sir."

I stand with my back to him and look out the window. I say very loudly, "And now—get out of here."

He leaves with a bow. I remain alone. Is it possible that I'm being followed?

MAY 6

We meet in Kuntsevo along the railroad bed: Vanya, Heinrich, Fyodor, and me. They are wearing high boots and caps, like peasants.

I say, "On the fourteenth the governor-general is going to the theater. We need to agree on our posts. Who will throw the first bomb?"

Heinrich becomes agitated. "I want to be first."

Vanya has light brown hair, grey eyes, and a pale forehead. I regard him questioningly.

Heinrich repeats, "I insist on being first, I insist."

Vanya smiles affectionately, "No, Heinrich, I've been waiting a long time. Don't be angry: it's my turn. I want to be first."

Fyodor puffs his cigarette indifferently.

I ask, "Fyodor, what do you think?"

"Well, I'm always ready."

Then I say, "The governor-general will probably go through Spassky Gate. Vanya will be at Spassky, Fyodor at the Trinity, and Heinrich at Borovichi. Vanya will throw the first bomb."

Everyone remains silent.

The narrow rails stretch along the railroad bed. The telegraph poles recede into the distance. It's quiet. Only the buzz of the telegraph wires is audible.

"Listen," says Vanya. "Here's what I've been thinking. It's easy to make a mistake. The bomb weighs four kilos. You throw it by hand—you can't be sure to hit your target. If, for example, you hit the rear wheel—then he'll remain alive. You recall on the first of March, what happened with Rysakov."[37]

Heinrich becomes agitated. "Yes, yes . . . what shall we do?"

Fyodor listens attentively. Vanya says, "The best plan: throw the bomb under the horses' legs."

"Well?"

"Well, it would destroy the carriage and the horses."

"And you as well."

"And me."

Fyodor shrugs his shoulders with contempt. "There's no need for that at all. We'll kill him anyway. Run up to the window, and throw the bomb at the glass pane. That's all there is to it."

I look at them. Fyodor is lying on his back on the grass and the sun is burning his dark cheeks. He squints; he's delighted with spring. Vanya, pale, looks pensively into the distance. Heinrich paces back and forth and smokes intermittently. Above us is the blue sky.

I say, "I'll tell you when to sell your carriages. Fyodor will dress as an officer, and you, Vanya, as a doorman; you, Heinrich, will stay as a peasant in your jacket."

Fyodor turns his head to me. He's satisfied. He laughs, "You say, I'm being promoted. That's smart; almost a gentleman."

Vanya says, "George, we still have to consider the bombs."

I stand up. "Rest easy. I remember everything."

I shake hands with all of them. Heinrich catches up to me on the road. "George?"

"Yes, what?"

37. Nikolai Ivanovich Rysakov (1861–1881) was a Russian revolutionary and a member of the People's Will. He personally took part in the assassination of Tsar Alexander II, throwing a bomb that disabled the tsar's carriage. A second bomb by an accomplice killed the tsar. Rysakov was promptly arrested, put on trial, and hanged along with other accomplices.

"George . . . how can this be? How can Vanya do it?"

"He'll do it."

"That means he'll perish."

"He will."

He looks down at his feet, at the grass. There are traces of our feet on the fresh grass. "I can't abide that," he says hoarsely.

"What can't you?"

"That . . . that he's the one to do it." He pauses. He says quickly, "It's better if I go first. I'll perish. How will it be if they hang him? They will, won't they? Hang him?"

"Of course they'll hang him."

"Well, then, I can't abide it. How will we live if he dies? Let them hang me."

"And then they'll hang you, too, Heinrich."

"No, George, listen, no. . . . Can you imagine that Vanya will be gone? Here we are calmly deciding, and as a result of our decision Vanya will certainly perish. The main thing is that it's certain. No, for God's sake, no . . ." He plucks his beard. His hands tremble. I say, "Here's what, Heinrich, one of these two: this way or that. Either it's the terror, and then cease all these boring conversations, or keep talking, and go back to the university."

He's silent. I take hold of his arm. "Remember, General Togo said to his Japanese:[38] 'I regret only one thing, that I have no children who could share your fate with you.' Well, we should regret one thing, that we can't share Vanya's fate. There's nothing to cry about."

Moscow is close by. The Arch of Triumph is sparkling in the sun. Heinrich raises his eyes, "Yes, George. You're right."

I laugh, "You just wait: *suum quique*."[39]

---

38. Marshal-Admiral Marquis Tōgō Heihachirō (1848–1934) was a *gensui*, or admiral of the fleet, in the Imperial Japanese Navy and one of Japan's greatest naval heroes.

39. A Latin phrase often translated as "to each his own" or "may all get their due."

MAY 7

Erna comes into my room, sits down in the corner, and begins to smoke. I don't like it when women smoke. I feel like telling her about it.

"Will it be soon, Georgie?" she asks.

"Soon."

"When?"

"On the fourteenth, Coronation Day."

She wraps herself in a warm shawl. Only her blue eyes can be seen. "Who will be first?"

"Vanya."

"Vanya?"

"Yes, Vanya."

I find her large hands unpleasant, as well as her affectionate voice and her red cheeks. I turn away. She says, "When should I prepare the bombs?"

"Wait a bit. I'll tell you."

She goes on smoking for a long time. Then she stands up and paces the room in silence. I look at her hair. It's flaxen and it curls on her temples and forehead. How could I have kissed her?

She pauses. She looks into my eyes timidly. "You believe in our success, don't you?"

"Of course."

She sighs. "May God help us."

"And you, Erna, don't you believe in it?"

"No, I do."

I say, "If you don't believe—then leave us."

"But Georgie, dear. I do believe."

I repeat, "Leave me."

"George, what's wrong?"

"Ah, nothing. For God's sake, leave me in peace."

She hides in the corner again and wraps herself in her shawl once more. I don't like these women's shawls. I remain silent.

The clock on the mantelpiece is ticking. I'm afraid: I wait for her complaints and tears.

"Georgie."

"What, Erna?"

"No. It's nothing."

"Well then, goodbye. I'm tired."

In the doorway she whispers sadly, "Goodbye, dear." Her shoulders droop. Her lips tremble.

I feel sorry for her.

MAY 8

They say that where there are no laws, there's no crime. What is my crime if I kiss Elena? How am I to blame if I don't want to see Erna any longer? I ask myself. I find no answer.

If I had laws, then I wouldn't kill, probably wouldn't kiss Erna, and wouldn't look for Elena. But what does my law consist of?

Moreover, they say it's necessary to love one's fellow man. But if there's no love in one's heart? They say it's necessary to respect him. But if there's no respect? I'm on the border of life and death. What do I care for words about sin? I can say about myself: "And I looked, and behold a pale horse: and his name that sat on him was Death."[40] Wherever this horse sets his hooves, the grass withers; and wherever the grass withers, there is no life, and therefore, no law. For death knows no law.

MAY 9

Fyodor sold his equipage in the horse market. He's an officer now, a cornet in the dragoons.[41] His spurs jingle and his saber clinks on the pavement. He looks taller in his uniform and his gait is more self-assured and steadier.

---

40. Revelation 6:8. See above, first epigraph to the novel.

41. A low rank in the Russian cavalry.

He and I are sitting together in Sokolniki Park on a dusty platform. The violin bows are singing in the orchestra. Military uniforms flash before us, as well as ladies' white dresses. The soldiers salute Fyodor. He says, "Listen: how much do you think that outfit costs?" He points at one well-dressed lady at the next table.

I shrug my shoulders. "I don't know. Perhaps about two hundred rubles."

"Two hundred?"

"Yes."

Silence.

"Listen."

"What, Fyodor?"

"When I worked I used to get a silver ruble a day."

"Well?"

"Well, nothing."

Electric lights come on. A frosted globe shines quite low over our heads. Blue shadows streak the white tablecloth.

"Listen."

"What, Fyodor?"

"What do you think, if, as an example, we did in these people?"

"Did what?"

"Well, a bomb."

"What for?"

"So that they knew."

"Knew what?"

"That working people are dying like flies."

"Fyodor, that's anarchism."

"Anarchism? What a word.... This attire cost two hundred rubles, while children beg for kopecks. How about that?"

I find it strange to see his silver shoulder straps, his white military jacket, and his white cap band. It is strange to hear these words.

I say, "Why are you angry, Fyodor?"

"Hey, there's no justice in this world. We work day in and day out in the factory, our mothers wail, our sisters walk the streets . . . and these people . . . pay two hundred rubles. . . . No. We should do them all in with a bomb, without doubt."

The bushes are getting lost in the darkness, the forest is growing uncannily dark. Fyodor rests his elbows on the table and keeps silent. There's malice in his eyes. "We should do them all in with a bomb, without doubt."

MAY 10

There are only three days left. In three days the governor-general will be killed. The imperishable will perish.

Elena's image is obscured by fog. I close my eyes; I want to resurrect it. I know: she has black hair and black eyebrows; she has slender arms. But I don't see her. I see a dead mask. Nevertheless, a secret belief lives in my soul: she will be mine again.

It makes no difference to me now. There was a thunderstorm yesterday; I heard the first clap of thunder. Today the grass looks clean and the lilacs are in bloom in Sokolniki. The cuckoo cries at sunset. But I don't notice the spring. I've almost forgotten about Elena. Well, let her love her husband; let her not be mine. I'm alone. I'll remain alone.

That's what I tell myself. But I know, a few days will pass and in my thoughts I will be with her again. Life will pass in an orderly cycle. If only these days will pass quickly.

Today I was walking along the boulevard. There was still a smell of rain in the air, but the birds were already chirping. To the right, on the wet path next to me, I noticed a man. He was a Jew, and he was wearing a bowler hat and a long yellowish coat. I turned into the narrow lane. He stood on the corner and watched me for a long time.

I ask myself again: am I being followed?

MAY 11

Vanya is still a cabdriver. He came to meet me still wearing his holiday clothes. We're sitting on a bench in the square near Christ the Savior Cathedral.

"Georgie, the end has come."

"Yes, Vanya, the end."

"I'm so glad. How happy and proud I'll be. You know, my whole life seems like a dream to me. As if I were born to die and . . . to kill."

The cupolas of the white cathedral reach to the sky. Down below the river glistens in the sun. Vanya is serene. He says, "It's difficult to begin to believe in miracles. But if you do come to believe, there are no further questions. Why then is there violence? Why the need for a sword? Why blood? Why 'Thou shalt not kill'? But we have no faith. A miracle, they say, is a fairy tale for children. But listen and tell me whether it's a fairy tale or not. Perhaps it's not a fairy tale at all, but the truth. Listen."

He takes out a Gospel bound in black leather. On the front cover is a gilded cross.

"'Jesus said: Take ye away the stone. Martha, the sister of him that was dead, saith unto Him, Lord, by this time he stinketh: for he hath been dead four days.

"'Jesus saith unto her, Said I not unto thee, that, if thou wouldst believe, thou shouldst see the glory of God?

"'Then they took away the stone from the place where the dead was laid. And Jesus lifted up his eyes and said, Lord, I thank thee that thou hast heard me.

"'And I knew that thou hearest me always: but because of the people which stand by I said it, that they may believe that thou has sent me.

"'And when he thus had spoken, he cried with a loud voice, Lazarus, come forth.

"'And he that was dead came forth, bound hand and foot with grave clothes; and his face was bound about with a napkin. Jesus saith unto them, Loose him and let him go.'"[42]

Vanya closes his Gospel. I say nothing. He repeats, lost in reflection, "'Lord, by this time he stinketh: for he hath been dead four days.'"

Swallows are circling in the blue air. In the monastery across the river bells are ringing for vespers. Vanya says in a whisper, "You hear, Georgie, four days . . ."

"Well?"

"A great miracle."

"And Serafim of Sarov—is that also a miracle?"[43]

Vanya doesn't hear me. "George."

"What, Vanya?"

"Listen. 'But Mary stood without at the sepulcher weeping: and as she wept, she stooped down, and looked into the sepulcher.

"'And seeth two angels in white sitting, the one at the head and the other at the feet, where the body of Jesus had lain.

"'And they say unto her, Woman, why weepest thou? She saith unto them, Because they have taken away my Lord, and I know not where they have laid him.

"'And when she had thus said, she turned herself back, and saw Jesus standing, and knew not that it was Jesus.

"'Jesus saith unto her, Woman, why weepest thou? Whom seeketh thou? She, supposing him to be the gardener, saith unto him, Sir, if thou have borne him hence, tell me where thou hast laid him, and I will take him away.

"'Jesus saith unto her, Mary. She turned herself and saith unto him, Rabboni; which is to say, Master.'"[44]

---

42. John 11:39–44.
43. Serafim of Sarov (1754 or 1759–1833), born Prokhor Moshnin, is one of the most renowned Russian saints in the Eastern Orthodox Church. He is generally considered the greatest of the nineteenth-century *startsy* (elders). He was canonized in 1903.
44. John 20:11–16.

Vanya falls silent. It is quiet. "Did you hear, George?"

"I did."

"Is that really make-believe? Tell me."

"Vanya, do you believe?"

He says from memory, "'But Thomas, one of the twelve, called Didymus, was not with them when Jesus came.

"'The other disciples therefore said unto him, We have seen the Lord. But he said unto them, Except I shall see in his hands the print of the nails, and put my finger into the print of the nails, and thrust my hand into his side, I will not believe.

"'And after eight days again his disciples were within, and Thomas with them: then came Jesus, the doors being shut, and stood in the midst and said, Peace be unto you.

"'Then saith he to Thomas, Reach hither thy finger, and behold my hands; and reach hither thy hand, and thrust it into my side; and be not faithless, but believing.

"'And Thomas answered and said unto him, My Lord and my God.

"'Jesus saith unto him, Thomas, because thou hast seen me, thou hast believed: blessed are they that have not seen, and yet have believed.'[45] Yes, George, 'blessed are they that have not seen, and yet have believed.'"

The day is waning and the spring coolness is descending. Vanya shakes his curly head. "Well, Georgie, goodbye. Farewell forever. Be happy." There is sadness in his clear eyes. I say, "Vanya, what about 'Thou shalt not kill'"?

"No, Georgie. Kill."

"What are you saying?"

"Yes, I say, kill so that no one else kills later. Kill, so that people will live according to God's will, so that love sanctifies the world."

"That's blasphemy, Vanya."

"I know. And 'Thou shalt not kill'—isn't that blasphemy?" He extends both his hands to me. He gives me a big, bright smile.

45. John 20:24–29.

And suddenly he kisses me warmly, like a brother. "Be happy, Georgie."

I kiss him, too.

MAY 12

I had a meeting today with Fyodor at the Siu Confectionary.[46] We discussed details of the attempt on the life of the official.

I left the place first. I noticed three detectives standing at a neighboring gate. I recognized them by their furtive eyes and anxious glances. I paused at the shop window. I turned into a detective myself. I followed them like a bloodhound. Were they after us or not?

Then Fyodor left the shop. He calmly walked along Neglinnaya Street. Immediately one of the spies, a tall redhead, wearing a white apron and a soiled cap, rushed to a cab. The two others ran after him. I tried to catch up with Fyodor and wanted to stop him. But he took a fast cab that just happened by. They all raced after him—like a pack of angry dogs. I was sure that he was done for.

I didn't remain alone either. All around me were some very odd people. There was a man wearing someone else's overcoat. His head was lowered and his red hands were crossed behind his back. There was a lame man in tatters, a beggar from the Khitrov Market. There was my recent acquaintance, the Jew. He was wearing a top hat and had a trimmed black beard. I realized that I was going to be arrested.

The clock struck twelve. I had a meeting with Vanya at one in Georgievsky Lane. Vanya hadn't yet sold his equipage. He's still a cabdriver. I secretly hope he'll drive me away.

I walk to Tverskaya Street. I want to get lost in the crowd, to dissolve in the sea of people. But the same figure appears again in front of me: his arms folded behind his back, his feet tripping on the

46. One of the oldest and largest confectionaries in Moscow.

hem of his long coat. And once again alongside the dark Jew in the top hat. I noticed: he didn't let me out of his sight.

I turn into the lane. Vanya isn't there. I walk to the end of it and then turn around abruptly. Someone's eyes are fixed on me. Someone was following me with sharp eyes, someone quick-moving was following my every step.

I'm on Tverskaya once again. I remember: at the corner there's a door leading to the lane. I start running. I hide behind the gates. I press my back up against the wall and freeze. Several minutes pass—they seem like hours. I know that the dark Jew is close by. He's the lookout. He's waiting. He's the cat and I'm the mouse. It's four paces to the doorway. I cock the trigger on my Browning revolver, measuring the distance with my eyes. All of a sudden—with one jump I'm in the lane. Vanya's driving slowly to meet me. I rush to him. "Vanya, hurry up!"

The wheels rattle on the pavement; the springs creak at the turns. We turn the corner. Vanya whips his horse. I turn back: the street is empty at the bend. No one's there. We got away.

And so, there's no doubt: we're being followed. But I don't lose hope. What if this is merely a coincidence? If they don't know who we are? If we manage to carry out our plan? If we're able to kill him?

But then I remember Fyodor. What happened to him? Has he been arrested?

MAY 13

Fyodor is waiting for me in Sofiika at the Bear Restaurant. I must see him. If he's surrounded, our affair is done for. If he's managed to escape, we can hold out until tomorrow and then we will succeed.

I'm sitting at a table in the tavern near the window. I can see the street, a policeman in his soaking wet cloak, a driver with his enclosed cab, and the umbrellas of the occasional passerby. Rain is beating down on the windowpanes, gloomily pouring off the roof. It's grey and dull.

Fyodor enters. His spurs jingle; he greets me. On the street familiar figures appear in the rain. Two of them, burying their wet faces in the collars, guard the entrance. Two more are standing with the policeman on the corner. One of them is the lame fellow from yesterday. I search for the Jew. There he is, of course—under the carved awning over the gate.

I say, "Fyodor, we're being followed."

"What?"

"Followed."

"That's impossible."

I take hold of his sleeve. "Well then, just look."

He stares intently out of the window. Then he says, "Look, that lame fellow, like a sodden mutt . . . yes, indeed . . . damn it . . . what are we going to do, George?"

The building's surrounded by police. We have little chance of escaping. We would be arrested on the street.

"Fyodor, is your revolver ready?"

"Revolver? I have eight cartridges."

"Well, friend, let's go."

We descend the staircase. A doorman in his livery politely opens the front door for us. My revolver is in my pocket, my finger on the trigger. At ten paces and we will hit the bullseye for sure.

We walk shoulder to shoulder. Fyodor's saber clanks. I know: Fyodor's ready for anything. I've been ready for a long time. Suddenly Fyodor nudges me with his elbow. He whispers rapidly, "Look, George, look." There's a lonely cabdriver on the corner. "Here's a speedy horse for you, sir."

"Five rubles for your tip. Get a move on."

The prize trotter races ahead at a gallop. Clods of mud fly into our faces. A sheet of rain stretches across the sky. From somewhere behind us we can hear a voice yelling, "Stop!"

Thick steam is rising from the horse. I shake the driver by the shoulder. "Hey, driver, faster. Another five-ruble tip."

In the park we jump into the bushes. It is wet. The trees are dripping. Rain has washed out all the paths. We run through the puddles.

"Goodbye, Fyodor. Leave today for Tver."

His uniform flashes for a moment among the green bushes and then disappears. Toward evening I'm back in Moscow. I won't go to the hotel. The plan's completely spoiled. What's happened to Vanya? Heinrich? Erna?

I have no lodging and spend the long night wandering around Moscow. Time passes very slowly. It's still a long way until dawn. I'm tired and chilled and my feet ache. But there's hope in my heart. I still harbor hope within me.

MAY 14

Today I sent a note inviting Elena to a meeting. She came to meet me in the Alexander Garden. She has sparkling eyes and black curls. I say, "Great waters can't quench love and rivers can't drown it, because love is strong as death. Elena, say the word, and I'll abandon everything. I'll abandon the revolution, leave the terror behind. I will be your slave."

She looks at me with a smile. Then she says thoughtfully, "No."

I lean over close to her. I say in a whisper, "Elena . . . do you love him? Do you?"

She is silent.

"You don't love me, Elena?"

Suddenly with a strong movement she extends her long, slender arms to me. She embraces me. She whispers, "I love you, I love you. I love you."

I hear her words and I feel her body. Intense joy flares in me and I say with effort, "I'm going away, Elena."

"Where to?"

"To Petersburg."

She turns pale. I look her right in the eye. "Listen, Elena. You don't love me. You don't know me. If you did love me, you'd be worried about me. I'm being followed. I'm hanging by a hair. Perhaps I'll be hanged tomorrow. But it doesn't matter to me: you don't love me."

She asks anxiously, "You said you're being followed?"

The evening wind is whispering indifferently; it smells like rain. There's no one in the park. We're alone. I say loudly, "Yes, I'm being followed."

"George, dear, leave here at once, immediately."

I laugh, "And don't come back?"

She says, "I love you, George."

"Don't make fun of me. How dare you talk about love? Is that really love? You're living with your husband and I'm an outsider to you. Can you really love me?"

"I love you, George."

"You love me? But you're living with your husband."

"Ah, my husband . . . don't talk about him."

"But do you love him? Do you?"

But once again she makes no reply.

Then I say to her, "Listen, Elena. I love you and I will return. And you will be mine. Yes, you will."

She embraces me again. "Dearest, I am with you; I'm yours."

"And his? Yes, his, too?"

I leave. Evening fades. The streetlights shine with a yellow light. Anger's stifling me. I say to myself: "His and mine, mine and his. And his, his, his."

MAY 15

Today in the newspapers appeared the following:

During the course of the last week preparations were discovered by the Department of the Secret Police concerning an attempt on the life of the Moscow governor-general, which attempt was supposed to take place on the fourteenth day of May at the conclusion of the divine liturgy in the Assumption Cathedral. As a result of the measures taken, the criminal gang did not succeed in carrying out its nefarious plan; the conspirators have managed to escape and up to now have not been apprehended. Measures have also been taken to locate them.

I was amused by "measures taken." Haven't we taken our own measures? Victory is still not ours, but does that mean a defeat? The governor-general, of course, is still alive, but then so are we. Fyodor, Erna, and Heinrich have already left Moscow; Vanya and I leave today. We'll come back. Our word is law, and we'll take our revenge.

He who leads the people to captivity will also end up in captivity. He who draws a sword will also die by the sword.[47] That is written in the book of life. We will open it and remove the seal: the governor-general will be killed.

47. A reference to Matthew 26:52, "For all they that take the sword shall perish with the sword."

PART TWO

JULY 4

Six weeks have passed and I'm in Moscow once again. I have spent these weeks living in a house belonging to an old gentry family. From the white gates I can see a stripe: a green road lined with young birch trees. Yellow fields border the road on both sides. The rye whispers, and oats droop their heavy heads. In the noonday heat I will lie down on the soft earth. The ears of corn stand like an army and the poppies are bright red. It smells of clover and fragrant sweet pea. Clouds lazily melt away. A hawk soars lazily in the clouds. It flaps its wings smoothly and pauses in the sky. The whole world pauses with it: the heat and the black dot above.

I follow it intently with my eyes. And I recall the following lines from memory:

> . . . All nature, like a fog,
> Is overcome by a sultry doze,

And now the great god Pan
Slumbers peacefully in the nymphs' cave.[1]

But in Moscow there's acrid dust and stench. A line of carters drags along the dusty streets. The wheels rumble heavily. Heavy horses pull heavy loads. Open carriages bump along. Street organs drone. The bells of the streetcars resound. There's cursing and shouting.

I wait for nightfall. At night the town will fall asleep and the human surge subsides. And at night hope will once again shine forth: I'll give you the evening star.[2]

JULY 6

I'm no longer an Englishman. I'm a merchant's son, Frol Semenov Titov, timber merchant from the Urals. I'm staying in nasty rooms in Maroseika Street and on Sundays I attend mass in the parish Church of the Life-Giving Trinity. The most experienced eye won't recognize me as George O'Brien. The most experienced detective won't suspect that I'm a revolutionary.

There's a dirty tablecloth on the table in my room; a broken chair stands near the table. A faded geranium sits on the windowsill and portraits of tsars hang on the wall. In the morning the dirty samovar hums and doors slam in the corridor. I'm all alone in my cage.

Our first failure produced anger in me. The governor-general is still alive. Previously I also desired his death, but now anger floods me. I live with him inseparably. I can't close my eyes at night: I whisper his name; in the morning—my first thought is of him. There he is, the grey-haired old man with the pale smile on his bloodless lips. He despises us. He seeks our death. Power lies in his hands.

1. From a lyric titled "Noon" (1827–1830) by the Russian nature poet Fyodor Tyutchev (1803–1873).
2. See above, p. 4.

I hate his handsome palace, the carved coat of arms on the gates, his coachman, his guard, his carriage, and his horses. I hate his gold eyeglasses, his steely eyes, his sunken cheeks, his bearing, his voice, and his gait. I hate his wishes, his ideas, his prayers, his idle life, and his well-fed, clean children. I hate the man himself—his belief in himself, his hatred of us. I hate him.

Erna and Heinrich have already returned. I'm waiting for Vanya and Fyodor. It's quiet in Moscow; they've forgotten us. On the fifteenth, his name day,[3] he's going to the theater. We'll kill him along the way.

JULY 10

Andrei Petrovich has arrived from Petersburg once again. I see the lemon color of his face, his wedge-shaped grey beard. He's embarrassed as he stirs his tea with a teaspoon. "Have you read, George, they've disbanded the Duma?"

"I have."

"Yes. So much for a constitution. . . ." He's wearing a black tie, and an old-fashioned, dirty frock coat. He holds a cheap cigar between his teeth. "George, how are things?"

"What things?"

"You know . . . concerning the governor-general."

"Things are fine."

"It seems to be taking a long time. . . . You ought to move now. It's the right time."

"If it's taking a long time, Andrei Petrovich, then you hurry up and do it."

He is embarrassed and drums his fingers on the table. "Listen, George."

"Well?"

3. The feast day of a saint after whom a person is named.

"The Committee's resolved to intensify the terror."

"Well?"

"I say: in light of the disbanding of the Duma it's been resolved to intensify the terror."

I remain silent. We're sitting in a dirty tavern called Progress. The gramophone is rumbling hoarsely. The aprons of the waiters appear white in the blue smoke.

Andrei Petrovich says politely, "Tell me, George, are you satisfied?"

"Satisfied with what, Andrei Petrovich?"

"Well . . . with this increase."

"With what?"

"My goodness . . . I told you: the intensification of terror." He's sincerely glad to afford me pleasure. I laugh. "The intensification of terror? What of it? God willing."

"What do you think of it?"

"Me? Nothing."

"What do you mean, nothing?"

I stand up. "Andrei Petrovich, I'm pleased by the decision of the Committee, but I don't intend to intensify the terror."

"But why, George? Why?"

"Try it yourself."

He spreads his arms in surprise. He has dry, yellow hands, and his fingers are stained with tobacco. "George, are you joking?"

"No, I'm not joking."

I leave. Most likely he sits over his glass of tea a long time, pondering the question: wasn't I perhaps laughing at him and hadn't he offended me? I say to myself again: "Poor old fellow, poor grown-up child."

JULY 11

Vanya and Fyodor are already in Moscow. I've settled all the details with them. The plan remains the same. In three days, on the fifteenth of July, the governor-general will go to the Bolshoi Theater. The proceeds from the performance will go to the commission for wounded warriors. He can't possibly miss this performance in the theater.

Erna will hand me the explosives at seven o'clock. She will prepare them in the hotel on her own. She has the casings and dynamite in her room. She will dry the mercury over the spirit lamp, solder the glass tubes, and insert the fuse. She works well. I'm not afraid of an accidental explosion.

At eight o'clock I'll distribute the bombs. Vanya will stand at the Spassky Gate, Fyodor at Trinity, and Heinrich at Borovichi. We're not being followed now. I'm certain of that. In other words, power has been given to us: a sharp sword.

There's a bouquet of withered lilacs on my table. The green leaves have drooped; the pale pink flowers have faded. I search in the faded flowers for one with five petals—for good luck. And I'm glad when I find it, for luck is on the side of those who dare.

JULY 14

I recall: I was in the north, above the Arctic Circle, in a Norwegian fishing village. There were no trees, no bushes, not even grass. Bare cliffs, grey sky, and the gloomy, grey ocean. Fishermen in leather jackets were hauling in wet nets. It smelled of fish and blubber. Everything around seemed strange. The sky, the cliffs, the blubber, and these people with their strange language. I lost myself. I was a stranger to myself.

And today everything seems strange. I'm in Tivoli, opposite the open-air stage. The bald conductor is swinging his baton; the flutes in the orchestra are warbling sadly. Acrobats in pale pink tights appear on the well-lit stage. Like cats they climb up posts and then with all their might jump, do somersaults in the air, fly over one another, and, shining brightly in the dark night, confidently grab hold of the trapeze. I look at them apathetically, at their firm and flexible bodies. What am I to them and what are they to me? The crowd is passing by drearily, their feet crunching the sand underneath. Shop assistants with curled hair and well-fed merchants wander lazily around the garden. Out of boredom, they drink vodka, abuse each other, and laugh in boring fashion. The women greedily seek something with their eyes.

The evening skies grow dark; nighttime clouds gather. Tomorrow is our day. The clear idea, sharp as steel, arises in me. The idea of the murder. There is no love, no peace, and no life. There is only death. Death is the crown, the crown of thorns.

JULY 16

It was stifling yesterday from morning onward. The trees in Sokolniki Park were glumly silent. It felt as if there would be a thunderstorm. The first peal of thunder came from behind a white cloud. A black shadow settled on the earth. The tops of the fir trees began to murmur; a cloud of yellow dust arose in the air. Rain pelted the leaves noisily. The first blue bolt of lightning flashed timidly in the sky.

At seven o'clock I meet with Erna. She is dressed like a lower-class woman. She is wearing a green skirt and a white knitted shawl. Her disobedient curls are sticking out from beneath her shawl. In her arms she carries a large basket with linen.

The bombs are in this basket. I place them carefully in my briefcase. The heavy briefcase makes my arm ache.

Erna sighs. "Are you tired?" I ask.

"No, it's nothing. Georgie . . . may I go with you, Georgie?"

"No, Erna. It's not possible."

"George, dear—"

"No. Impossible."

There's timid entreaty in her eyes. I say, "Go home. At twelve midnight come back here to this place."

"George—"

"Erna, it's time."

It's still wet; the birch trees tremble, but the evening sun already glows in the sky. Erna's sitting alone on the bench. She'll be alone until nightfall.

At exactly eight o'clock Vanya's at the Spassky Gate, Fyodor at Trinity, Heinrich at Borovichi. I wander around the Kremlin. I wait for his carriage to drive up to the palace.

The lanterns of a carriage suddenly shine in the darkness. Glass doors slam. A grey shadow flashes on the white staircase. Black horses walk slowly around the entrance and proceed slowly at a trot. The chimes sound in the tower. . . . The governor-general is already at the Borovichi Gate. . . . I stand next to the monument of Alexander II.[4] The statue of the tsar rises above me in the darkness. The windows of the Kremlin palace glow with light. I wait.

Minutes pass. Days pass. Long years pass.

I wait.

The darkness is thicker, the square is even darker, the tower, higher, the silence, deeper.

I wait.

The chimes sound again.

I make my way to the Borovichi Gate. Heinrich is standing on Vozdvizhenka Street. He is wearing a blue jacket and his cap. He stands motionless on the bridge. He holds the bomb in his hands.

"Heinrich."

"George, is that you?"

"Heinrich, he's gone by. . . . The governor-general has driven past you."

"Past me?" He turns pale. His dilated eyes gleam feverishly.

"Where were you? Yes, where were you?"

"Where? I was here . . . at the gate."

"And you didn't see him?"

4. Alexander II (1818–1881) was tsar from 1855 until his assassination in 1881.

"No."

We stand under the dim light of the streetlamp. The flame was burning evenly.

"George."

"Well?"

"I can't . . . I'll drop it. . . . Take . . . the bomb . . . hurry up."

I almost yank the bomb out of his hands. We stand thus under the gaslight and look into each other's eyes. We both stay silent. The chimes sound for the third time.

"I'll see you tomorrow."

He waves his arm in despair. "Until tomorrow."

I return to my room. There's noise in the corridor, drunken voices. The lilacs are wilting. I tear the faded leaves off automatically. I search for floral happiness again. But my lips whisper on their own, "A living dog is better than a dead lion."[5]

JULY 17

In an agitated state, Heinrich says, "At first I was standing right next to the gate. . . . I stood there for about ten minutes. . . . Then I see: a policeman's noticed me. I started walking along Vozdvizhenka Street. . . . I turned back. I stood there. There was no sign of the governor-general. . . . I walked away again. . . . And that was probably when he drove past." He covers his face with his hands, "What a disgrace. What shame."

He didn't sleep a wink that night. He has blue shadows under his eyes and red blotches on his cheeks. "George, you believe me, don't you?"

"I do."

Pause.

I say, "Listen, Heinrich, why are you engaged in this terror? If I were you I would do some peaceful work."

5. Ecclesiastes 9:4.

"I can't."

"Why?"

"Ah, why? Is terror necessary or not? It is. You know that it's necessary."

"So what if it's necessary?"

"Then I can't refuse to go. What right do I have to refuse? Why, it's impossible to call for terror, talk about it, wish for it, and not do anything about it myself. . . . That's not possible. Is it?"

"Why is it impossible?"

"Ah, why? Well, I don't know; perhaps others can do it. . . . I can't." He covers his face with his hands again, and whispers once more, as if in a dream, "My God, my God . . ."

Pause.

"George, tell me truthfully: do you believe me or not?"

"I said: I believe you."

"And you will give me the bomb again?"

I remain silent.

He says slowly, "No, you'll give it . . ."

I remain silent.

"Well, then . . . then . . ." There's fear in his voice. I say, "Calm down, Heinrich, you'll get your bomb."

And he whispers, "Thank you."

At home I ask myself: Why is he engaged in terror? Whose fault is it? Isn't it perhaps mine?

JULY 18

Erna's complaining. She says, "When will all this be over, George? When?"

"What are you talking about, Erna?"

"I can't live for murder. I can't. . . . It has to be over. The sooner, the better."

Four of us are sitting in a room at a grimy tavern. There are names traced on the dirty mirrors and an out-of-tune piano stands near the window. Behind the thin partition someone is playing a maxixe.[6]

It's hot, but Erna is wrapped in a shawl. Fyodor is drinking beer. Vanya has placed his pale arms on the table and rests his head on his hands. Everyone is silent. Finally Fyodor spits on the floor and says, "Haste makes waste. You see, that devil Heinrich—the holdup is because of him."

Vanya raises his eyes, "Fyodor, aren't you ashamed? Why say that? Heinrich isn't to blame in any way. We're all guilty."

"Well then, all of us . . . but in my opinion, in for a penny, in for a pound."

Pause. Erna says in a whisper, "Ah, good Lord . . . isn't it all the same who's right and who's to blame? The main thing is to put an end to it. . . . And I can't. I can't."

Vanya kisses her hand tenderly. "Erna, dear, you're distressed. . . . And Heinrich? What about him?"

The maxixe continues on the other side of the wall. A drunken voice sings couplets.

"Ah, Vanya, what about Heinrich? I can't go on living. . . ." And Erna begins to sob.

Fyodor frowns. Vanya falls silent. And I feel strange: what good is this despair and why seek consolation?

JULY 20

I lie with my eyes closed. Street noise comes in through the open window; the stone city is sighing heavily. Half asleep, I see in my dream: Erna's preparing bombs.

Now she locks the door; the lock clicks softly. She slowly ap-

6. A dance, sometimes called Brazilian tango, that originated in Rio de Janeiro in 1868.

proaches the table and slowly lights the spirit lamp. There is light grey dust on the cast iron board: fulminate of mercury.[7] Thin blue tongues of flame—like serpents' fangs—seem to lick the iron. The explosive powder is drying. The little grains litter and crackle. The small leaden load moves along the glass. This load breaks the vent tube. Then there'll be an explosion.

One of my comrades already perished doing such work. They found his body in a room—or, pieces of his body: his splashed brains, bloodied chest, lacerated arms and legs. They loaded all this in a cart and took it to the police station. Erna's risking the same thing.

Well, and what if she should really be blown up? If instead of her flaxen hair and astonished blue eyes there remains only red flesh? Then Vanya will prepare the bombs. He's also a chemist. He will know how to carry out this work.

I open my eyes. A ray of summer sunshine has broken through the curtain and is shining onto the floor. I fall back half asleep. And I have the same thoughts. Why didn't Heinrich throw the bomb? Yes, why didn't he? Heinrich is not a coward. But a mistake is worse than fear. Or was it only chance? Was it his majesty Chance?

It doesn't matter—it's all the same to me. Suppose I'm to blame for Heinrich's taking part in the terror. Suppose he's to blame that the governor-general is still alive. Suppose Erna is blown up. Suppose both Vanya and Fyodor are hanged. No matter what, the governor-general will be killed. That's what I want to happen. I get up. On the square below my window people are rushing around like black ants. Each one is busy with his own business, petty cares of the day. I despise them. Wasn't Fyodor right in essence when he said, "Wish they all could be finished off with a bomb, with no exception."

7. A primary explosive, highly sensitive to friction and shock, used mainly as a trigger for other explosives in percussion caps and blasting caps.

JULY 21

Today I unintentionally wound up near Elena's house. Heavy and dirty, it looks out at the square. As is my habit, I search for a bench on the boulevard. As is my habit, I keep track of the time. As is my habit, I whisper: "I will meet her today."

When I think about her, for some reason I recall a strange southern flower. A plant of the tropics, the burning sun, and the scorched cliffs. I see the hard leaf of a cactus, the zigzag of its stem. In the middle of its sharp needles is a dark red scarlet flower. It's as if a drop of warm blood spurted forth and dried purple. I saw this flower once in the south, in a strange, dusty garden, among palm trees and orange groves. I stroked its leaves; its needles tore my hands; I leaned my face over to it and inhaled the heady, sharp, intoxicating fragrance. The sea was sparkling, the sun was shining at its zenith, and a magic spell was being cast. The red flower bewitched and tortured me.

But I don't want Elena now. I don't want to think about her. I don't want to remember her. I'm possessed by revenge. And I no longer ask myself if revenge is worth it.

JULY 22

Twice a week the governor-general travels to his office, from three to five o'clock, in his house on Tverskoi Boulevard. He goes by different routes on different days. We'll keep track of his departure and will occupy all the roads in a day or two. Vanya will await him on Tverskaya, Fyodor at Stoleshnikov Lane. Heinrich will wait in reserve: he'll remain further off, behind the palace. This time we can hardly fail.

What would I be doing if I were not involved in terror? I don't know. I don't know how to answer that question. But I know one thing for certain: I don't want to live a peaceful life.

Opium smokers have blissful dreams; they see bright groves of paradise. I don't smoke opium and don't have blissful dreams. But what's my life without terror? What's my life without struggle, without the joyful awareness that worldly laws are not for me? And in addition I can say, "Thrust in thy sickle and reap: for the time has come for thee to reap."[8] It is time to reap those who are not with us.

JULY 25

I say to Fyodor, "You, Fyodor, take up your post at Stoleshnikov Lane, from the square to Petrovka. The governor-general will probably take the route where Vanya's waiting, but you should also be ready. And remember: I'm counting on you."

He took off his dragoons uniform some time ago and is now wearing a cap of the Ministry of Justice. He's clean shaven and his black mustache curls upward. "Well, George, he'll really get it this time."

"You think so?"

"Certainly. This time he won't get away."

We're in the outskirts of Moscow, in the Neskuchnyi Garden.[9] A white palace is hidden among the thick green linden trees. The governor-general has been staying here recently.

Fyodor says thoughtfully, "Those scoundrels live in quite some quarters. They sleep peacefully, eat sweetly . . . damned gentry . . . well, fine: just wait—soon there'll be a funeral mass."

"Fyodor . . ."

"What?"

"If you're going to be tried, don't forget to hire defense counsel."

"Defense counsel?"

"Yes."

---

8. Book of Revelation 14:15.

9. The oldest park in Moscow, dating from the eighteenth century.

"That is, a lawyer of some kind?"

"Well, yes, a lawyer."

"I don't need a lawyer. . . . I don't like them, those lawyers. . . . And there won't be a trial. . . . What are you thinking? I don't need a trial. . . . I'll fire the last bullet into my head, and that will be the end of it."

I know that for a fact by his voice: he'll fire the last bullet into his own head.

JULY 27

Sometimes I think about Vanya, his love, his words, so full of his belief. I don't believe in these words. For me they're not my daily bread and not even a rock. I can't understand how one can believe in love, love God, and live for the sake of love. And if it weren't Vanya who was saying these words, I would laugh. But I'm not laughing. Vanya could say this about himself:

Tormented by spiritual thirst
I dragged myself through a somber desert.
And a six-winged seraph
Appeared to me at the crossing of the ways.[10]

And this, too:

He clove my breast with a sword,
And plucked out my quivering heart,
And thrust a coal of live fire
Into my gaping breast.

Vanya will die. He'll no longer exist. The "coal of live fire" will be extinguished with him. And I ask myself: what's the difference between him and Fyodor, for example? They'll both kill. They"ll

10. This and the following stanza come from Alexander Pushkin's famous lyric "The Prophet" (1826).

both be hanged. They'll both be forgotten. The difference is not in their deeds, but in their words.

And when I think like that, I laugh.

JULY 29

Erna says to me, "You don't love me at all. . . . You've forgotten me. . . . I'm a stranger to you."

I say reluctantly, "Yes, you're a stranger to me."

"George . . ."

"What, Erna?"

"Don't talk like that, George." She doesn't cry. Today she's calm. I say, "What are you thinking about, Erna? Is this the time to think? Just look: failure after failure."

She repeats in a whisper, "Yes, failure after failure."

"And you want love? I have no love now."

"Do you love another woman?"

"Perhaps."

"No, tell me."

"I told you a long time ago: I love another woman."

She leans her whole body toward me. "It doesn't matter. Love whomever you wish. I can't live without you. I'll love you forever."

I look into her sad blue eyes. "Erna."

"George, dear . . ."

"Erna, you had better go."

She kisses me. "George, I don't want anything; I'm not asking for anything. Just be with me sometimes."

Night falls softly above us.

JULY 31

I said: I don't want to remember Elena. Nevertheless, my thoughts are with her. I can't forget her eyes: they hold the midday light. I can't forget her hands, her long, transparent pink fingers.

The soul of a person is in their eyes and their hands. Can there really be an ugly soul in a beautiful body? But suppose that she's not joyful and proud, but a slave? What follows from that? I want her; there's no one better, no one more joyful, no one stronger. Her beauty and her strength are in my love.

Sometimes there are dark and misty summer evenings. A turbid, milk-white fog rises from the dew-soaked earth. The bushes melt in its warm waves; vague outlines of the forest dissolve. The stars twinkle faintly. The air is thick and damp and smells of new-mown hay. These are nights when the meadow spirit hovers silently above the swamp.[11] He casts his spell.

Here's another spell: why do I care about Elena, her carefree life, her officer husband, her future as a wife and mother? Meanwhile I'm bound to her with an iron chain. I lack the strength to break the chain. But is it really necessary to break it?

AUGUST 3

Tomorrow's our day again. Erna will prepare the bombs again. Fyodor, Vanya, and Heinrich will occupy their assigned positions again. I don't want to think about tomorrow. I'd say I'm afraid to think about it. But I'm waiting for it and I believe in it.

AUGUST 5

Here is what happened yesterday:

At two o'clock I took the bombs from Erna. I said goodbye to her on Tverskaya and met Heinrich, Fyodor, and Vanya on the boulevard. Fyodor took up his post on Stoleshnikov Lane, Vanya on Tverskaya, and Heinrich at some distant lanes.

I dropped into Filippova's Cafe, ordered a glass of tea for myself, and sat down near a window. It was stuffy. Wheels rumbled on

11. A figure from Russian folklore.

the cobblestones; the roofs of houses were exhaling heat. I waited a short time, perhaps five minutes. I recall: suddenly amid the loud noise of the street came a heavy, unexpectedly loud and full burst of sound. It was as if someone had struck a hefty blow with a cast iron hammer against a cast iron bar. And immediately there came the distressing crash of broken glass. Then all was quiet. On the street a noisy crowd of people ran down into Stoleshnikov Lane. A ragged lad was shouting something in a loud voice. Some old woman with a basket in her arms threatened with her fist and cursed. Doormen came running out of gateways. The Cossacks galloped past. Somewhere someone said, "The governor-general's been killed."

With difficulty I made my way through the crowd of people swarming in the lane. It still smelled of thick smoke. Shards of glass were scattered on the pavement, as well as black pieces of broken wheels. I realized that the carriage had been destroyed. In front of me, blocking the road, stood a tall workman wearing a blue shirt. He waved his bony arms and was saying something quickly and excitedly. I wanted to push him away to see the carriage close up, but all of a sudden, somewhere on the right, I heard sharp gunshots being fired one after another in a nearby lane. I rushed off in that direction. I knew that Fyodor was shooting. The crowd pressed against me, almost crushing me in its soft embrace. Shots rang out again, now further away, shorter and fainter. Once more everything was quiet. The factory worker turned his face to me and said, "Just look at that, he keeps firing . . ."

I grabbed his arm and pushed him back forcefully. But the crowd closed in tighter in front of me. I saw the backs of heads, some beards, some broad backs. Suddenly I heard the words, "The governor-general's alive . . ."

"Did they catch them?"

"I haven't heard whether they did . . ."

"They'll catch them. . . . How could they not?"

"Yes. . . . There are so many of them nowadays . . . of these . . ."

I returned home late that night. I remembered only one thing: the governor-general was still alive.

AUGUST 6

The following was published in today's newspapers:

Yesterday a villainous attempt was carried out on the life of the governor-general. At three o'clock the governor-general left the Kremlin palace for his office on Tverskaya Street. His Excellency's adjutant, Lieutenant Prince Yashvil, who usually draws up the schedule for the route, this time relayed the proposed route to the town governor: through the Spassky Gate along Red Square through Petrovka and Stoleshnikov Lane to the governor-general's house. When the horses turned off Petrovka, a man wearing the uniform of the Ministry of Justice emerged onto the pavement. In one hand he held a box tied with a ribbon, the way boxes of candy are usually tied. Having drawn near the carriage, he took the box into both his hands and threw it under the wheels. There followed a deafening explosion. Fortunately the governor-general remained alive. After getting up from the ground without any assistance, he headed for the entrance to the house of the merchant Solomonov, where he remained until the arrival of a convoy, summoned by telephone. The Adjutant Prince Yashvil was thrown onto the left side of the road. His face was injured, both legs were crushed, and both arms were hurt. He died on the spot. The governor-general's coachman, the peasant Andreev, was severely wounded in the head. He died on arrival at the hospital. The assassin, after committing his villainous crime, began to run. The policeman on duty, Ivan Fyodorenko, and an agent from the Department of Secret Police, Ignaty Tkach, ran after him. The assassin fired two successive shots, killing his pursuers. After turning onto Petrovka, he tried to flee in the direction of Strastny Boulevard. Another policeman at his post, Ivan Klimov, attempted to stop him, but was badly wounded by a bullet fired into his stomach. On Petrovka the assassin jumped into a horse-drawn cab; threatening the driver with his gun, he forced him to drive to the Petrovsky Lines, where he resumed running down the lines. Here he was stopped again by the inspector of the first police district, Lieutenant-Colonel Orbeliani, and the doormen of houses No. 16, 18, and 20 on Petrovka. After firing two shots and killing two of the the aforementioned doormen, the assassin disappeared in the courtyard of house No. 3 along Petrovsky Line. The house was immediately surrounded by foot and horse police and a battalion of the Twenty-Third Grenadiers, summoned by telephone. During a search of the residential premises the assassin was discovered in a far corner of the courtyard, behind piles of firewood. He responded to a call to surrender by firing more shots, one of which killed Lieutenant-Colonel Orbeliani. Then the town governor, who was present at the site, ordered the Grenadiers to open fire on the assassin. Hiding behind the firewood, the assassin responded for some time with shots fired from his revolver; two soldiers, Velenchuk and Semenov, were slightly wounded; noncommissioned officer Ivan Edynak was killed. When the firing ceased, the Grenadiers discovered the body of the assassin behind the woodpile; it contained four bullet wounds, two of which certainly turned out to be fatal. The assassin was a young man, about twenty-six years old, tall and well built. No documents were found on him; in his trouser pockets were found two Browning revolvers and a box of cartridges.

Measures have been taken to ascertain his identity. The investigation is being led by a detective for extremely important affairs.

AUGUST 7

I am lying with my face buried in hot pillows. It's growing light. Dawn is breaking.

Another failure. Worse than failure, a catastrophe. We're utterly defeated. Of course, Fyodor did what he could. Did he miss the carriage? Didn't he throw the bomb? Wasn't there an explosion?

I don't feel sorry for Fyodor; I don't even regret that I wasn't able to defend him. Well, I might have killed another five doormen and policemen. Is that what I wanted to happen? But here's what I do regret: I didn't know that the governor-general was only two steps away from me, standing in the entry. I would have waited for him. I would have killed him.

We're not leaving. We won't give up. If we can't kill him in the street, we'll get into the palace. We'll blow up the whole palace, both ourselves and him, and everyone who's with him. He's calm now: he's rejoicing in his victory. He has no worries and no fears. His reign is secure, his power, firm.... But our day will come—the day of judgment. And then—it will be accomplished.

AUGUST 8

Heinrich says to me, "George, all is lost."

Blood rushes to my cheeks. "Shut up!"

Frightened, he takes a step back. "George, what's the matter with you?"

"Shut up! What nonsense. Nothing's lost. You should be ashamed."

"And Fyodor?"

"What about him? Fyodor was killed ..."

"Oh, George ... but that's ... that's ..."

"Well ... go on."

"No ... just think ... no ... but it seemed to me ... what now?"

"What do you mean?"

"The police are looking for us."

"The police are always looking."

It's drizzling. The sullen sky is weeping. Heinrich is soaking wet; water is streaming down from his worn cap. He's grown thin and his eyes have sunk into his head. "George."

"What?"

"Believe me ... I ... I merely want to say ... now there are two of us: Vanya and me ... two aren't enough."

"There are three of us."

"Who's the third?"

"Me. You forgot me."

"Will you carry the bomb?"

"Of course."

Pause.

"George, it's hard to do it on the street."

"What's hard?"

"It's hard to kill on the street."

"We'll go to his palace."

"His palace?"

"Yes. What surprises you?"

"You still hope, George?"

"I'm certain. . . . You should be ashamed, Heinrich."

Embarrassed, he shakes my hand heartily. "George, forgive me."

"Of course. . . . But remember: if Fyodor's killed, now it's our turn. Do you understand? Yes?"

And he whispers in agitation, "Yes."

But at that moment I was sorry that Fyodor was no longer with me.

AUGUST 9

I forgot to light the candles. Grey twilight fills my room. I see Erna's tremulous silhouette in the corner.

After the explosion I gave her the bombs and since then I haven't seen her. She furtively stole into my room today and kept silent. She wasn't even smoking.

"George . . ."

"What, Erna?"

"It's . . . it's my fault."

"What's your fault?"

"That he wasn't killed." Her voice is hollow and there are no tears today.

"Your fault?"

"Yes, mine."

"How?"

"I made the bomb."

"Oh, that's nonsense. . . . Don't torture yourself, Erna."

"No, it's me, it's me, it's me."

I take her hand. "Erna, it's not your fault. I'm telling you."

"No? And Fyodor?"

"What about Fyodor?"

"He might still be alive . . ."

"Erna, this is boring."

She stands up and takes two steps. Then she sits down again heavily. I say, "Now Heinrich said we should give it all up."

"Who said?"

"Heinrich."

"Give it up? Why?"

"Ask him, Erna."

"George, is it really true—should we give it all up?"

"Is that what you think? Yes?"

"No, you speak."

"Well, of course not. Of course we'll kill him. And you'll make the bombs again."

She says with alarm, "But who's the third?"

"Me, Erna."

"You?"

"Well, yes. Me."

She drops her head and presses her face to the window. She looks into the dark square. Then she suddenly stands up and approaches me. She kisses me warmly on the lips. "George, dear . . . shall we die together? George?"

Night falls quietly upon us again.

AUGUST 11

There are only two paths before us. The first: wait a few days and intercept him on the street once again. The second path: go to the palace. I know they're looking for us. It's hard for us to spend a week in Moscow, even more difficult to occupy the same positions. Well, instead of Fyodor—there's me, Vanya will be on Tverskaya again, and Heinrich will be in reserve. The police are now on alert. The streets are filled with detectives. They're on the lookout for us.

Suspecting a bomb, they may surround us and seize us by surprise. And besides, will the governor-general travel by the same route? Why, it would be easy for him to circle Moscow, exit on Tverskaya Street at the top, near Strastny Monastery . . . well, and if we go to the palace? We have to fasten the dynamite to ourselves, put on invisible armor, force our way into the entrance, and finally, blow ourselves up skillfully. Of course, I don't feel sorry for those who'll die: the family will perish, the servants, detectives, and the convoy. But it's dangerous to risk it. The palace is large and has many rooms. What if at the time of the explosion he's in the inner rooms or outside in the garden? We're not strong enough to reach him. . . . Khalturin's explosion was well planned and it ended in failure.[12] I am vacillating. I weigh all the pros and cons. I don't know: should we go to the palace? It's difficult to decide yet necessary to do so. It's hard to know and harder to find out.

AUGUST 13

Vanya is now a gentleman: he wears a soft hat, a light-colored tie, and a grey jacket. His hair is curly as before and his pensive eyes sparkle. He says, "Georgie, I'm sad that we lost Fyodor."

"Yes, indeed."

He smiles gloomily. "You're not sad that we lost Fyodor."

"What do you mean, Vanya?"

"Why, you're sorry that we lost a comrade. Isn't that so? Tell me, isn't it?"

"Of course."

"You think: there was a revolutionary, a genuine revolutionary, fearless . . . and now he's no longer alive. And you think: it's hard—how will we do without him?"

"Of course I do."

---

12. Stepan Nikolayevich Khalturin (1857–1882), a Russian revolutionary and member of the People's Will, was responsible for an unsuccessful attempted assassination of Alexander II of Russia.

"There, you see . . . but you've forgotten about Fyodor. You're not sorry about him personally."

A military orchestra is playing on the boulevard. It's Sunday. Workers are strolling in their red shirts, holding concertinas in their hands. There's talk and laughter.

Vanya says, "Listen, I keep thinking about Fyodor. For me, he was not only a comrade, not only a revolutionary . . . just think what he felt hiding there behind the woodpile. He kept shooting and he knew, with every drop of his blood he knew: death was imminent. How long did he stare it in the face?

"Georgie, not that. That's not what I mean. Of course he wasn't afraid. But do you know his agony? Do you know his torment once he was wounded? When the light was fading in his eyes and his life was burning out? Have you thought about that?"

I reply, "No, Vanya, I haven't."

He whispers, "That means you didn't love him either . . ."

Then I say, "Fyodor died. . . . It would be better if you said: should we go to the palace?"

"To the palace?"

"Yes."

"What do you mean?"

"Well, blow up the whole palace."

"And the people?"

"What people?"

"His family, his children."

"Is that what you're on about? Nonsense. It serves them right."

Vanya falls silent. Then: "George."

"What?"

"I don't agree."

"Agree with what?"

"To go to the palace."

"What rubbish. . . . Why not?"

---

13. John 5:43.

"I don't agree to kill children." And then he says in agitation, "No, George, listen to me: don't do this, no. How can you take that on yourself? Who gave you the right? Who allowed you?"

I say coldly, "I allowed myself."

"You?"

"Yes, me."

His entire body is trembling. "George, children . . ."

"So be it."

"George, what about Christ?"

"What does Christ have to do with this?"

"George, remember: 'I am come in my Father's name and ye receive me not; if another shall come in his own name, him ye will receive.'"[13]

"Why are you citing texts, Vanya?"

He shakes his head. "Yes, you're right. It's no use . . ."

We both remain silent for a long time. Finally I say, "Well, all right. . . . We'll do it on the street." His face lights up with a big smile. Then I ask him, "Perhaps you think I changed my mind because of the text you cited?"

"No, certainly not, George."

"I decided there's less risk that way."

"Of course, there's less risk, of course. . . . And you'll see: we'll succeed. God will hear our prayers."

I leave. I'm annoyed. Still, wouldn't it be better to go to the palace?

AUGUST 15

My thoughts are with Elena once again. I ask myself: Who is she? Why isn't she looking for me? How does she live without knowing anything about me? That means she doesn't love me. That means she's forgotten me. That means she was lying when she kissed me. But eyes like those don't lie.

I don't know. I don't want to find out anything. I have seen the joy of her love, heard the happy words. I want her and I will go and take her. Perhaps it's not even love. Perhaps tomorrow her eyes will fade and I'll be bored by the laughter that's so dear to me today. I love her today and what do I care about tomorrow? She appears before me now as if she were real: her black braids, the stern oval of her face, the timid glow of her cheeks. I call her; I say her name to myself. But soon our day will come, sure to be the last one . . .

Will I see her sometime or not?

AUGUST 17

Tomorrow we will await the governor-general on the street again. If I could, I would pray.

AUGUST 18

Erna has prepared the bombs for the third time. Precisely at three o'clock we're at our posts. I have the bomb in my hands. As I walk along, the fuse shakes steadily inside the box. I wrapped the box in paper and tied it with thin cord. It's as if I am coming from a shop with my purchase.

I proceed down the street on the left side of Stoleshnikov Lane. Autumn is in the warm air. I noticed this morning: there are already yellow leaves on some birch trees. Heavy clouds creep through the sky. A few drops of rain are falling.

I carry my bomb cautiously. If someone were to bump into me accidentally, the fuse would break. There are many spies on the sidewalks and on street corners. I pretend not to see them.

I turn back. It's quiet all around. The detectives lazily follow the passersby with their eyes. I'm afraid that the governor-general will drive past me at that very moment. It's hard to hurl the bomb now: I won't recognize his carriage and won't be able to prepare my strike. I feel for my revolver. I have two of them, just as Fyodor did. One is a Browning, and the other is a large Nagant, as carried by cavalrymen.[14] I cleaned them last night and carefully loaded them.

I walk up and down for half an hour. When I approach the corner of Tverskaya Square for the third time, near the wooden booth with the clock, I see: on Tverskaya near Vargin's house arising from the earth, a narrow column of yellow-grey smoke that's almost black at the edges. It broadens into a funnel above, filling the entire street. At that very moment—the familiar, strange, iron rumble. A cabman's horse on the corner rears up on its hind legs. In front of me there's a woman wearing a large black hat. She shrieks and sits down on the sidewalk. The policeman stands there for a second with a pale face and rushes toward Tverskaya.

I run toward Vargin's house. Broken windows crash. It smells of smoke again. I forget about the bomb; the fuse on it shakes steadily and quickly. I hear moans and shouts and I already know—I know for certain:

The governor-general has been killed.

An hour later they are selling extra editions of the newspaper. It has a black border and a cross. Under the cross—a photograph; under the photo—an obituary notice.

I hold the newspaper in my hands and my eyes grow dim.

AUGUST 20

Vanya managed to send us a letter from prison:

Contrary to my desire, I was not killed when I threw the bomb. I hurled it from a distance of three paces right into the window of the carriage. I saw the face of the governor-general. Having noticed me, he leaned back in the carriage and raised his hands to protect himself. I saw how the carriage was

14. The Nagant Revolver is a seven-shot, gas-seal revolver that was designed and produced by Belgian industrialist Léon Nagant for the Russian Empire.

destroyed. The smoke and glass shards flew at me. I fell on the ground. After I stood up, I looked around. About five paces away from me were scattered pieces of clothing; nearby lay the bloodied body. I wasn't hurt, although blood was flowing from my face and the sleeves of my jacket had been burned. I walked on. Just then someone's strong hands grabbed hold of me from behind. I didn't resist. They took me off to the police station.

I have fulfilled my duty—the duty of a revolutionary. I await my trial and will accept my sentence calmly. I think that even if I had managed to escape, I still wouldn't be able to live after what I did.

I embrace you, dear friends and colleagues. I thank you with all my heart for your love and friendship. I believe in the imminent revolution and will die with the proudest awareness of its victorious triumph.

In bidding you farewell, I would like to remind you of these simple words: "Hereby perceive we the love of God, because he laid down his life for us: and we ought to lay down our lives for the brethren."[15]

This letter included a postscript for me personally. Vanya wrote,

Perhaps you think it strange that I spoke of love and resolved to kill, that is, to commit the most serious sin against people and God.

I couldn't refrain from killing. If I had the pure and innocent faith of disciples, then of course I wouldn't have engaged in terror. I believe: the world will be saved not by the sword, but by love and it will be governed by love. But I didn't have in myself the strength to live in the name of love; and I realized that I can and should die in its name.

I feel neither repentance nor joy from what I have done. Blood torments me and I know: death is no redemption. But I also know: "I am the way, the truth, and the life."[16]

People will judge me and I pity that they will have to shed my blood. In addition to their judgment, I believe, will also come God's judgment. My sin is infinitely large, but Christ's mercy knows no limits.

I kiss you. Be happy, happy in truth and in deed. And remember: "He that loveth not knoweth not God; for God is love."[17]

---

15. 1 John 3:16.
16. John 14:6.
17. 1 John 4:8.

I keep rereading these leaves of cigarette paper and I ask myself: perhaps Vanya is right. No, the warm sun is shining today; the falling leaves in Sokolniki Park are rustling. . . . I wander along familiar paths and a great radiant joy burns inside me. I pluck some autumn flowers, inhale their vanishing scent, and I kiss their pale petals. It seems like Easter; prophetic words resound with triumphant resurrection: "And there came a great voice out of the temple of heaven, from the throne, saying, It is done."[18]

I am happy: yes, it is done.

18. Book of Revelation 16:17.

PART THREE

AUGUST 22

I'm still hiding out here in Moscow, still unable to leave. The police are on the lookout: they're searching for us persistently. I gave up my rooms in the hotel and have changed my disguise for the third time. I'm no longer Frol Semyonov, nor the Englishman George O'Brien. I live invisibly—without a name and without a home. During the day I wander around Moscow; toward nightfall I search for lodging. I spend the night wherever I can: today in a hotel, tomorrow on the street, the day after with some strangers whom I don't even know—merchants, civil servants, or priests. Sometimes I laugh maliciously: my hosts' faces reflect fear, timid respect for me.

Autumn advances. The old park gleams like gold; leaves rustle beneath my feet. At dawn the puddles covered with the thin glass of brittle ice glisten in the sunlight.

I love the sad autumn. I sit on a bench in Sokolniki Park listening to the forest. The quiet peace envelops me. It seems to me that there is no murder and no blood. There is only the sacred earth for everyone and the sacred sky above.

An iron grate encircles the place where Vanya killed. Behind the grate there are crosses and an icon case. People hurry past. A passerby pauses infrequently; an old woman crosses herself. An officer salutes casually.

The murder has already been forgotten. Only the police remember; and of course, we remember. Vanya is being tried. There will be speeches and silences; he'll be sentenced and hanged.

Life will come to an end.

AUGUST 23

I summoned Elena today by letter. She enters and at once I feel joyful and serene. It's as if there weren't any long days of anxiety and expectation, as if it weren't me living with revenge, coldly preparing the killing. That feeling of joy and serenity sometimes occurs on summer evenings, when the stars have started to sparkle and there's the fragrance of flowers in the garden, warm and heady.

Elena is wearing a white dress. She radiates freshness and good health. She's twenty years old. Here eyes are not laughing; bashful, she asks, "Have you been in Moscow all this time?"

"Yes, of course I've been in Moscow."

"So you . . . ?"

"What?"

"So then . . . it was you?" She lowers her eyes.

I feel like embracing her warmly, lifting her in my arms, kissing her like a child. Now, as I see her, her shining eyes, I know: I love her childish laughter, the innocent beauty of her life. I listen to her voice with ecstasy: "My God, if you only knew how frightened I was. When it happened, I already knew that . . . it was you . . . that you . . . were victorious." And then she adds in a whisper, "How awful . . ."

And then I think: *I was living by the thought of her, but she wasn't thinking about me, wasn't suffering for me. She was thinking about the terror, about the fact that I was killing. Yes, of course I was killing. . . .* I say aloud, "Yes, we are the ones who did it."

She blushes. And suddenly, as she did then, she places her hands on my shoulders softly and tenderly. Her breath burns my face. Our lips meet with unknown anguish.

I recover my senses—she's sitting in an armchair. Her kiss is still on my lips and she's so near and yet a stranger.

"George, dear, beloved George, don't be sad." And she moves toward me bashfully and warmly.

I kiss her. I kiss her hair and her eyes, her pale fingers, her beloved lips. I'm no longer thinking about anything else. I know only: she's here in my arms; her young body is trembling.

The fading glow of sunset shines in the window. A red ray wanders across the ceiling. She lies in my arms, white, and I no longer feel the aftereffect of spilled blood.

There is nothing at all.

AUGUST 24

Erna leaves today. She's grown thin and somehow looks faded. The red color in her cheeks is gone but as before her hair is helplessly curly, as if asking for mercy. I'm saying farewell to her for what will be a long time.

She stands before me, fragile and sad. Her lowered eyelashes are trembling. She says softly, "Well, Georgie, this is the end."

"Are you glad?"

"Are you?"

I want to tell her that I'm happy and proud, but today in my soul I feel no rejoicing. I remain gloomily silent.

She sighs. Under the lace of her dress her breast heaves deeply and fitfully. Apparently she wants to say something to me; she's agitated and doesn't dare speak. I say, "When does your train leave?"

She shudders. "At nine o'clock."

I look at my watch with indifference. "Erna, you'll be late."

"George . . ." She still can't decide. I know: she'll start talking about love and will ask for sympathy in return. But there's no love in me and I can't help her in any way.

"George, is it really true?"

"Is what true?

"Are we really going to part?"

"Ah, Erna, it's not forever."

"No, it is forever." Her voice is barely audible. I answer her loudly, "You're tired, Erna. Get some rest and forget."

Her whisper reaches me, "I won't forget."

At that minute I can see: her eyes have turned red and copious tears are streaming softly down her face, like water. She shakes her head unattractively. Locks of her hair are wet with her tears and hang down pitifully to her neck. She sobs and whispers incoherently, swallowing her words, "George, dear, don't leave me. . . . My sweetheart, don't leave me . . ."

An image of Elena arises in my memory. I hear her resonant, joyful laughter; I see her sparkling eyes. And I say coldly to Erna, "Don't cry."

She falls silent at once. She wipes her tears and looked out the window desolately. Then she stands and approaches me unsteadily. "Farewell, George. Farewell."

I repeat like an echo, "Farewell."

She stands next to my open door and waits. And she still whispers with distress, "George, you will come . . . George?"

AUGUST 28

Erna left. In addition to me, Heinrich's still in Moscow. He'll follow Erna. I know: he loves her and, of course, he believes in love. I find it amusing and annoying.

I remember: I was in prison and expecting to be executed. The prison was damp and dirty. It smelled of cheap tobacco and soldier's cabbage soup in the corridor. A guard was walking back and forth under my window. Sometimes fragments of life, haphazard words of conversation, would drift in through the wall. It was strange:

there outside the window were the sea, sunshine, and life, while here inside were loneliness and inevitable death. . . . During the day I would lie on an iron cot and read last year's *Niva*.[1] In the evening lamps twinkled dimly. I would climb onto the table stealthily, gripping the iron bars with my hands. I could see the dark sky and the southern stars. Venus was shining brightly. I kept saying to myself: *There are still many days ahead, morning will still dawn; there will be days and nights. I will see the sun and I will hear people.* But somehow I didn't believe in death. Death seemed unnecessary and therefore impossible. There was not even any joy or serene pride that I was dying for the revolution. There was only some strange indifference. I didn't feel like living, nor did I want to die. The question of how my life was lived didn't trouble me; doubts about what lies beyond the dark boundary did not arise. But I do recall: would the rope cut into my neck and would suffocation be painful? Often in the evening, after the roll call, when the drums had grown quiet in the courtyard, I stared intently at the yellow light of the lamp—the single item on the prison table covered with crumbs. I would ask myself: is there no fear in my soul? And I would answer myself: no. Because it was all the same to me, all the same. . . . And then I escaped. During the first days there was only the same dead indifference in my heart. I automatically did everything so that I wouldn't be caught. But why I did that or why I had escaped—I don't know. There in prison it sometimes seemed to me that the world was beautiful and I yearned for air and warm sunshine. But then, once free, I was plagued again by boredom. But then one time, toward evening, I remained alone. The east had already grown dark and the early stars were twinkling. The mountains were veiled in violet mist. A night breeze blew from the river below. There was a strong smell of grass. The cicadas were droning loudly. The air was thick and sweet, like cream. And at that moment I suddenly understood that I was alive; there was no death; that life was once again before me, and that I was young, healthy, and strong . . .

1. The most popular magazine in late nineteenth-century Russia.

And now I feel the same way. Yes, I'm young, healthy, and strong. Once again I have escaped death. And for the hundredth time I ask myself: how am I to blame if I kissed Erna? And wouldn't I have been more to blame if I had turned away from her, or pushed her away? A woman came to me and brought love and nice affection. Why does this affection give rise to grief? Why does love afford not joy, but torment? I don't know; I can't and won't even try to find out. It sometimes seems to me that Vanya knows. But he's no longer with us.

SEPTEMBER I

Andrei Petrovich has come again. He had a hard time finding me and now he's shaking my hand heartily and with delight. His old face is beaming. He's content. The wrinkles around his eyes have spread into a smile. "I congratulate you, George."

"For what, Andrei Petrovich?"

He squints slyly and shakes his bald head. "On your victory and success."

I feel bored by him and would willingly leave. His words annoy me, his tiresome congratulations. But he's smiling at me innocently. "Yes, George, to tell you the truth, we were already losing hope. Failure after failure—we felt that they were your failures. And you know"—he leans closer to my ear—"they even wanted to dismiss you."

"Dismiss me? What do you mean?"

"It's a thing of the past. . . . I'll tell you, we didn't believe it would happen. So much time, but no results. . . . And we had begun to think: wouldn't it be better to dismiss him? No change; nothing would come of it . . . like old fools, eh?"

I regard him in astonishment. He looks the same: grey and decrepit. His fingers, as always, are stained by tobacco.

"And you . . . did you think we should be dismissed?"

"Now, George, you've already become angry."

"I'm not angry . . . but tell me—do you think we should be dismissed?"

He pats me affectionately on the shoulder. "Hey, you . . . one can't joke with you." And then he says in a businesslike manner, "Well, and now whom? Huh?"

"For now, no one."

"No one? The Committee has decided on the Minister of Justice."

"That's the Committee; as for me . . ."

"Ah, George."

I laugh. "What's wrong, Andrei Petrovich? I say, give us time."

He thinks to himself for a long time, chewing his lips like an old man. "George, will you stay in Moscow?"

"Yes, I will."

"It's better to leave."

"I have some business here."

"Business?" He looks sad: *What sort of business?* But he doesn't dare ask me. "Well, all right, George; come and we'll talk about it . . ." Once again he shakes my hand with delight. "That was very clever. Well done . . . good lads . . ."

Andrei Petrovich is a judge: he praises and he disapproves. I remain silent: He sincerely believes that I appreciate his praise. Poor old man.

SEPTEMBER 3

Vanya's being tried today. I'm lying on a couch in chance lodgings, my head resting on hot pillows. It's night. I can see the night sky framed in the window. A necklace of stars sparkles in the sky. The Great Bear.

I know: Vanya lay all day on his prison cot; sometimes he got up, went to the table, and wrote. And now the Great Bear is twinkling for him as it is for me. And just like me, he's not asleep.

I also know: tomorrow is his execution. Tomorrow the hangman wearing a red shirt will come with a rope and a whip. He will tie Vanya's hands behind his back and the rope will cut into his flesh. His spurs will clank under the vaults; the guards will present arms gloomily. The gates will open. . . . A warm mist rises on the sandy spit; feet sink into the wet sand. The east grows pink. A hooked black pole stands out against the pale pink sky. This is the gallows. This is the law.

Vanya climbs the platform. He looks grey in the morning mist; his eyes and hair are the same color. It's cold and he shivers, pulling his neck deep into his upturned collar. Then the hangman puts on the shroud and tightens the string. The shroud is white and the red executioner stands next to him. The stool is pushed away with an unexpected noise. The body swings. Vanya has been hanged.

The pillows burn my face. The blanket falls onto the floor. It's uncomfortable to lie here. I see Vanya, his enthusiastic eyes, his brown curls. I ask myself timidly: why the gallows? Why blood? Why death? And at once I recall, "We must lay down our lives for our brothers." That's what Vanya said. But Vanya's no longer with us.

SEPTEMBER 5

I say to myself: Vanya's no longer with us. These are simple words, but I don't believe in them. I don't believe that he's already dead. There might come a knock at the door, he'll come in quietly, and as before, I'll hear: "He that loveth not, knoweth not God, for God is love."[2]

Vanya believed in Christ; I don't. What's the difference between us? I lie, spy, and kill. Vanya lied, spied, and killed. We all live by deceit and blood. In the name of love?

Christ ascended Golgotha. He didn't kill; he gave people life. He didn't lie; he taught people the truth. He didn't betray; he himself was betrayed by a disciple. So, it's one of two choices: either the path to Christ or . . . or as Vanya said: Smerdyakov. . . . And in that case, I am Smerdyakov.

---

2. See above, p. 86.

I know: Vanya's death is sacred; his last truth was in suffering. That holiness and that truth are inaccessible to me, incomprehensible. I will die, as he did, but my death will be dark. Because there is wormwood in bitter waters.[3]

SEPTEMBER 6

Elena says to me, "You know, I was so afraid for you. . . . I dared not think about you. . . . You're so . . . strange."

We are in Sokolniki, as before. An autumn breeze stirred in the forest, driving crimson leaves in the wind. It's cold. It smells of earth.

"Dear, it's so nice . . ."

I take her hand, kiss her slim fingers, and my mouth whispers to her, "My dear, my dear, my dear . . ."

She laughs. "Don't be so sad. Be cheerful."

But I say, "Listen, Elena. I love you; I say: come away with me."

"Why?"

"I love you."

She presses her body close to mine and whispers, "You know—I love you, too."

"And your husband?"

"What about him?"

"You're with him."

"Ah, my dear . . . what difference does it make—now I'm with you."

"Stay with me forever."

She laughs heartily. "I don't know. I don't know."

"Elena, don't laugh and don't joke."

"I'm not joking." She embraces me again. "Must one love forever? Is it possible to love forever? You would like for me to love only you. . . . I can't. I'm going."

---

3. A reference to Book of Revelation 8:10–11.

"To your husband?"

She nods in silence.

"That means you love him."

"Dearest, the evening sun blazes, the wind murmurs, the grass whispers. And we love each other. What more is needed? Why think about what's been? Why think about what will be? Don't torment me. I don't need suffering. Let's rejoice together, let's live. I don't want grief and tears . . ."

I say, "You say that you're both his and mine. Tell me—is that so? Is it true?"

"Yes, it is." A shadow passes over her face. Her eyes are sad and dark. Her white dress is fading in the day's twilight.

"Why?"

"Ah, why?"

I leaned in close to her, "And if . . . if you didn't have a husband?"

"I don't know. . . . I don't know anything at all. . . . Does love last forever? Don't ask, my dear. . . . And don't think, don't think, don't think . . ." She kisses me; I stay silent. Jealousy slowly blossoms in my soul: I don't want to share her with anyone and I won't.

SEPTEMBER 10

Elena visits me in secret and the hours and weeks fly by like rushing water. The whole world for me now consists in my love for her. The scroll of reminiscences is sealed; the mirror of life is dimmed. Before me I see Elena's eyes, her lips, her loving hands, all her youth and her love. I hear her laughter, her joyful voice. I play with her hair; I greedily kiss her warm, happy body. Night falls. At night her eyes are even brighter, her laughter is heartier, her kisses more intense. And like a spell the vision reappears: a strange southern blossom, a blood-red cactus, enchanting and beloved. What do I care about the terror, the revolution, the gallows, and death if she is with me? She comes in timidly, her eyes lowered. But her cheeks are aflame with fire and her laughter rings out. Sitting on my knees, she sings lightheartedly and richly. What are her songs about? I don't know; I don't hear. I feel her entire being and her happiness resounds in my heart; there's no sadness left in me. She kisses me and whispers, "I don't care . . . if you leave tomorrow . . . but today you're mine. . . . I love you, dearest."

I can't understand her. I know: women love those who love them; they love love. But today it's her husband, tomorrow it's me, and the day after tomorrow it's his kisses once again. . . . Once I said to her, "How can you kiss two men?"

She raised her fine eyebrows. "Why not, my dear?"

I didn't know how to reply. I said with malice, "I don't want you to kiss him."

She burst out laughing. "And he doesn't want me to kiss you."

"Elena . . ."

"What, my dear?"

"Don't talk to me like that."

"Ah, my dear, my dear . . . what business is it of yours whom I kiss and when? Do I really know whom you've kissed before? Can I really want to know that? Today I love you. . . . Aren't you glad? Aren't you happy?"

I wanted to say to her: *You have no shame, no love*. . . . But I remained silent: is there any shame left in my soul?

"Listen," she said, laughing. "Why are you talking like this? Why say this is permitted, but that isn't? Know how to live, to be happy, to get love out of life. You don't need malice and you don't need murder. The world is large and there's enough joy and happiness for everyone. There's no sin in happiness. There's no deceit in kisses. . . . So don't think about anything and kiss me."

And then she said, "You, my dear, don't know what happiness is. . . . Your entire life is only blood. You're made of iron; the sun is not for you. . . . Why, why think about death? You must live joyfully. . . . Isn't that right, my dear?"

I made no reply.

SEPTEMBER 12

I'm thinking about Elena again. It may be that she doesn't love me and doesn't even love her husband. Perhaps she loves only love. Her radiant life exists only in love; she was born into the world for love and she will go to the grave in its name. And when I think like this, I experience a comforting malice. So what if Elena's with me, that I kiss her splendid body and see her sparkling, loving eyes? She leaves me to return to her husband with a smile; she lovingly shares his life. I'm troubled by the thought of him, this fair-haired, well-built young man. Sometimes in the quiet I catch myself having deep, secret daydreams. And then it seems to me that I'm not thinking about him, but about the person who no longer exists and about whom I felt malice previously. It seems to me that the governor-general is still alive.

I walk along a thorny way. He, her husband, stands on my narrow path. He hinders me: she loves him.

I look: tired autumn is declining in the gardens. The cold asters are glowing; dry leaves are falling. Morning frost covers the grass. On these days of decay the familiar idea arises clearly. I recall the forgotten words:

> If a louse in your shirt
> Shouts to you that you're a flea,
> Go out onto the street
> And—kill!

SEPTEMBER 13

Heinrich has been living in Moscow all this time. He has family in Zamoskvorechye. Only today is he leaving for Petersburg to join Erna. He's gotten some rest, filled out a bit, and grown stronger. His eyes sparkle and he no longer utters stale phrases. I haven't seen him for a long time.

We're sitting together in a tavern. At one time Vanya was sitting here with us. Heinrich is eating and between bites of food he says, "Have you read, George, what's being said in the *Revolutionary News?*"

"About what?"

"About the governor-general."

"No, I haven't read it."

He's angry and says passionately, "They write about the meaning of the event not merely in Moscow but in all of Russia. I agree: this act is a turning point. Now they'll see how strong we are; they'll realize that the party will be victorious, that it can't fail." He takes out a thin sheet of printed paper. "Here, George, read it."

I'm bored listening to him, and would be bored reading it. I push the paper away. I say with reluctance, "Put it away. It's not worth it."

"What do you mean? How can you say it's not worth it? All our work is for this."

"Whose work do you mean?"

"Our work, of course."

"For a newspaper article?"

"You're making fun of it. . . . A newspaper article is essential. Propaganda for terror is necessary. Let the masses understand; let the idea of struggle penetrate the countryside. Isn't that so?"

I'm bored. I say, "Let's not talk about this. Listen, Heinrich, you love Erna, don't you?" He drops his spoon into his plate and blushes deeply. Then he says in a trembling voice, "How do you know?"

"I know."

He falls silent in embarrassment.

"Well, then, take care of her. . . . I wish you happiness."

He stands up, paces the dirty room where we are. Finally he says softly, "George, I believe you. Tell me the truth."

"What do you want me to tell you?"

"You don't love Erna?"

I'm amused by his gloomy face covered in red blotches. I laugh loudly. "Me? Love Erna? What are you saying? Certainly not."

"And never . . . you never loved her?"

I say clearly and distinctly, "No. I never loved her."

His face beams with a happy smile. He shakes my hand heartily. "Well, I'm leaving. Goodbye." He leaves quickly. I sit there alone at the grimy table for a while, amid the dirty dishes. Suddenly it's all extremely funny: I love, she loves, he loves . . . what a tedious tale.

SEPTEMBER 14

I didn't see Elena today. I went to Tivoli in the evening. The orchestra was playing loudly and brazenly as always and the gypsies were singing. As always women were wandering among the tables, their silk dresses rustling. And I felt bored as I always do.

A drunken naval officer was sitting at the next table. Wine was sparkling in their glasses and the women's jewels were glittering. Their laughter and senseless chatter reached me. The hands on the clock were moving slowly.

All of a sudden I hear, "Why do you seem so bored here?" The officer, tottering, stretches out his wine glass to me. His cheeks are purple and his mustache is clipped short. The governor-general had a mustache like that. "Aren't you ashamed to be bored here? Allow me to introduce myself: Berg. . . . Join us, at our table. . . . The women are asking for you."

I stand and give my name: "Engineer Malinovsky."

I don't care where I sit: I sit down at their table lazily. Everyone laughs and clinks glasses with me. The violins are wailing and through the window I can see the dawn breaking. Suddenly I hear someone ask, "Where's Ivanov?"

"What Ivanov?"

"Lieutenant Ivanov. Where has Ivanov gone?"

I remember: Director of the Secret Police Ivanov. Isn't that what his name is? I lean my head to my neighbor's shoulder. "Excuse me, do you mean Colonel Ivanov of the gendarmerie?"

"Well, yes . . . of course . . . the very one. . . . He's my dear friend . . ."

A longed-for temptation burns within me. I won't stand up. I won't leave. I know: this Ivanov, of course, has my photograph with him. I feel for my revolver and I wait.

Ivanov arrives. He looks like a merchant, portly and wearing a reddish beard. He sits down at the table heavily and drinks some vodka. They introduce us, of course.

"Malinovsky."

"Ivanov."

He's come to drink and I feel bored once again. The longed-for temptation returns—to go up to him and to whisper, "George O'Brien, colonel."

But I stand up silently. Rain is seeping outside; the stone city is asleep. I'm alone. I feel the cold and darkness.

SEPTEMBER 15

I ask myself: why am I in Moscow? What can I achieve? Elena is only my lover. She'll never be my wife. I know this, but I still can't leave. I also know that every extra day involves extra risk and that my life is in danger. But that's what I want.

At Versailles, in the park, the lakes are visible from the veranda. Among the graceful groves and attractive flowerbeds their borders stretch in clear lines. The fountains are enveloped in mist; the mirrorlike waters remain still. A sleepy serenity hovers above us.

I close my eyes: I'm in Versailles. I'd like to forget about Elena; I'd like to enjoy peace today. The river of life is flowing. The day comes and goes. And I am like a slave in chains with my love.

Somewhere, far away, there is ice on the mountaintops. The mountains gleam blue, covered in virginal snow. People live in peace at the foot of the mountains; they love in peace and then die in peace. The sun shines for them; love warms them. But, in order to live as they do, one doesn't need anger or the sword. . . . I remember Vanya. Perhaps he was right, but the white robes are not for me: Christ is not with me.

SEPTEMBER 16

"My dear, why are you always so sad?" Elena says to me. "Don't I love you? Look here, I'll give you a pearl as a gift." She takes a ring off her finger. There's a large pearl, like a teardrop, set in a gold ring. "Treasure it. . . . It's my love." She embraces me trustfully. "You're sad because I'm not your wife. Oh, I know: marriage is a habit of love, stale; it's love without sparkle. But I want to love you. . . . I want beauty and happiness . . ."

And she says pensively, "Why do people inscribe various letters, compose words from those letters, and laws from those words? There are libraries full of those laws. Don't live, don't love, and don't think. There's a prohibition for every day. . . . It's ridiculous and foolish. . . . Why must I love only one person? Tell me, why?"

Once again I'm unable to reply.

"You see, George, you're silent. You don't know either. Have you never loved anyone else?"

I feel awkward. Yes, I've loved other women and I've never known why laws are written. She's repeating my own words. But now I feel that they're a lie. I want to tell her this, but I dare not.

She has heavy, dark tresses. They fall to her shoulders. In the dark frame of her curls her face is even paler and thinner. And her eyes await an answer.

I kiss her in silence. I kiss her innocent hands, her strong young body. My kisses torment me. Once again I have a bewitching thought—the thought of who else, like me, kisses her and whom she loves. I say, "No, listen, Elena . . . it's either him or me."

She laughs. "You see: I'm a slave and you're my master. . . . But what if I don't want to choose? Tell me: why I should choose?"

Rain can be heard forcefully outside the window. I see her silhouette in the semidarkness, her large eyes, which look black at night. And I say, growing pale, "That's what I want, Elena."

She remains silent and gloomy.

"Choose."

"I can't, dear . . ."

"I said: choose."

She stands up quickly. She says decisively and calmly, "I love you, George. You know that. But I will never be your wife."

She leaves. I'm alone. I have only her pearl ring.

SEPTEMBER 17

Elena loves her own splendid body, her young life. People say that there's freedom in this love. I find it amusing: let Elena be a slave and I a master; let me be a slave while she is free. . . . I know one thing for sure: I can't share love. I can't kiss her, if another man is also kissing her.

Vanya was searching for Christ. Elena's searching for freedom. It's all the same to me: let it be Christ, let it be the Antichrist, let it be Dionysus. I'm not searching for anything. I love. And my love is my right.

Once again the crimson flower is making me drunk. Once again the mysterious spell is at work. I'm like a stone in the desert. But in my hand I hold a sharp sickle.

SEPTEMBER 18

Yesterday was a day when something I was waiting for happened and something I secretly believed wouldn't happen. It was a day of sorrow and desecration. I was walking across the Kuznetsky Bridge. A milky fog was creeping up, melting in waves of mist.

I was strolling without a goal, without thoughts, like a ship in the waves, without a rudder.

Suddenly a spot thickened in the fog; a vague shadow wavered. An officer was walking rapidly straight toward me. He glanced at me and stopped immediately. I recognized him: Elena's husband. I stared into his eyes and could see the anger in his dark pupils.

Then I took his arm gently and said, "I've been waiting for you a long time."

We continued along Tverskaya Street in silence. We walked a long time in the mist and we both knew the way. We felt close to each other, like brothers. We emerged into the park.

It was autumn there. Bare branches—like prison bars. The fog was melting and the grass was being soaked by the mist. It smelled of decay and moss.

Deep in the park, in an overgrown thicket, I chose a path. I sat down on a stump of a felled tree and said coldly, "Did you recognize me?"

He nodded his head to me in silence.

"Do you know why I'm in Moscow?"

He nodded again.

"Well, you know: I won't leave."

He said with a smile, "Are you sure about that?"

Am I sure? I don't know. Who knows whom Elena loves? But I said only, "And you?"

Pause.

"Here's what: you leave Moscow. Do you understand? You."

He flushed with anger. But he said coldbloodedly, "You're mad."

Then I silently withdrew my revolver. I measured off eight paces on the grass and marked the barriers with wet reeds. He watched attentively. I finished. He said with a smile, "So, you intend to fight?"

"I demand that you leave."

Fair and well built, he looked me in the eye. He repeated sarcastically, "You're mad."

After a silence, I said, "Will you fight?"

He unfastened his holster, and unwillingly withdrew his revolver. Then he thought for a moment and said, "All right . . . I'm at your service."

A moment later he was standing at the barrier. I knew: I can hit an ace from a distance of ten paces. I couldn't miss.

I raised my revolver. I took aim at a button on his coat. I waited.

Silence. I said in a very loud voice, "One. . . ." He remained silent. "Two and . . . three."

He stood motionless, his chest facing me. His revolver was lowered. He was mocking me. . . . All of a sudden some hot and hard lump clutched my throat. I shouted to him angrily, "Shoot!"

Not a sound. Then I slowly, contentedly, pressed the trigger. There was a flash of yellow flame and a cloud of white smoke.

I walked across the wet grass and leaned over the body. He lay on the path face down in the cold, soft mud. His arm was bent in a strange manner, his legs stretched wide apart. It was drizzling. There was a mist. I turned into a grove in the forest. It was already twilight. It was pitch dark among the trees. I walked aimlessly, just like a ship without a rudder.

SEPTEMBER 20

Men are perishing senselessly in the Tsushima battle.[4] The night is dark, there is a mist at sea, and the waves are high. The battleship is hiding like a huge wounded beast. The black smokestacks are barely visible; the thundering guns are quiet. They fought during the day; they flee at night, awaiting an attack. Hundreds of eyes sweep the darkness. Suddenly there's a scream like the cry of a frightened seagull: "A torpedo-boat alongside." A searchlight flares, blinding the night with its white light. And then . . . whoever was on deck dives into the sea. Whoever was inside, behind the steel armor, beats against the hatch. The ship sinks slowly, nose first into the water. The machinists in the engine room drop down like sacks. Iron chains strike them, the wheels mangle them, the smoke chokes them, and the steam scorches them. Thus do they perish. A senseless death.

And then there is more death. The north, the sea, and a northern storm. Wind tears the sails, raising white foam. A fishing boat

4. See above, p. 13.

is being tossed in the grey waves. A grey day dissolves in pale twilight. Somewhere in the distance a lighthouse appears. Red, white, and then red again. Men are frozen on the slippery foredeck, clutching the ropes tightly. The waves roar and the rain splashes.... And suddenly, through the howling wind—the sound of a bell tolls slowly. A bell is clanging in the water on the low side of the boat. It's a buoy. It's a sandbank. It's death.... And then the wind comes once more, the sky, and the waves. But there's no one left.

And there's another death: I've killed a man.... Up to now I've been justified: I kill in the name of terror, for the revolution. Those who sank the Japanese knew what I know: death is necessary for Russia. But I killed for myself. I wanted to kill and I did. Who's the judge? Who condemns me? Who justifies me? I find my judges ridiculous, as well as their severe sentences. Who will come to me and say with genuine faith: Thou shalt not kill? Who will dare to throw a stone? There's no distinction, no difference. Why is it all right to kill for the terror, necessary to kill for the fatherland, but for oneself—impossible? Who will answer me?

Night is shining through the window; I see the gleaming stars. The Bear sparkles; the silver Milky Way streams, the Pleiades glimmer timidly. What's beyond them? Vanya believed. He knew. But I stand here alone and night remains incomprehensibly silent, the earth breathes a secret, and the stars twinkle mysteriously. I've walked a difficult path. Where is the end? Where's my well-deserved rest? Blood begets blood; vengeance lives by vengeance. I've killed not just him.... Where shall I go? Where shall I fly?

SEPTEMBER 22

Today it has been raining since morning, a light, autumn rain. I look at its spidery net and tedious thoughts trouble me languidly, like falling drops.

Vanya lived and died. Fyodor lived and was killed. The governor-general lived and is no longer. . . . Men live, die, and are born.

They live and die. . . . The sky grows gloomy and it pours down rain.

I feel no remorse. Yes, I killed. . . . I have no bitterness for Elena. It's as if my fatal shot burned up my love. Her torment is now foreign to me. I don't know where she is or how she's faring. Is she weeping over him, over her blameless life, or has she already forgotten him? Whom has she forgotten? Me? Me and him. Him again. We're chained to one another even now.

It's pouring rain and making noise on the iron roofs. Vanya said: how can one live without love? That's what Vanya said, not me. . . . No. I'm a master of the red guild.[5] I'll take up my trade once again. Day in and day out, long hour after hour, I will prepare to kill. I will follow stealthily, I will live by death, and a day will come with its intoxicating joy: it's been accomplished—I am victorious. And thus to the gallows, to the grave.

And people will praise, rejoice loudly in the victory. What do I care about their anger or their pitiful joy?

A milky white fog has once again enveloped the whole town. The chimneys protrude gloomily; a prolonged whistle sounds from the factory. A cold mist creeps up. It's pouring rain.

SEPTEMBER 23

Christ said: "Thou shalt not kill," and His disciple Peter unsheathed his sword in order to kill. Christ said: "Love one another," and Judas betrayed Him. Christ said: "I have come not to judge, but to save," and He was judged.

Two thousand years ago He prayed, sweating blood, while his disciples were asleep. Two thousand years ago people dressed Him in a purple mantle: "Take Him and crucify Him." And Pilate said: "Shall I crucify your king?" But the high priests replied, "We have no king but Caesar."

5. That is, the revolutionaries.

And we have no king but Caesar. And now Peter still unsheathes his sword; Annas judges with Caiaphas;[6] Judas, son of Simon, betrays. And now they are still crucifying Christ.

That means that He is not the vine and we are not the branches. That means that His word is but an earthen vessel. That means that Vanya was not right. . . . Poor, loving Vanya . . . he was looking for a justification of life. Why did he need that?

The Huns have come through the fields and trampled the green shoots. The pale horse has stepped on the grass and the grass withered. People have heard the Word—and the Word has been defiled.

Vanya wrote with faith: "The world will be saved not by the sword, but by love, and love will be established." Yet Vanya also killed, "having committed the greatest sin against men and God." If I thought as he did, then I would not have been able to kill. And, having killed, I am not able to think as he did.

As for Heinrich: there are no riddles for him. The world is as simple as the alphabet. On one side there are slaves, on the other—masters. The slaves revolt against their masters. It's right if a slave kills. It's wrong if a slave is killed. There will come a day when the slaves are victorious. Then there will be paradise and the joyful ringing of bells on earth: everyone will be equal, well fed, and free.

I don't believe in paradise on earth; I don't believe in paradise in heaven. I don't want to be a slave, even a free slave. My entire life is a struggle. I can't refrain from it. But I don't know in whose name I am struggling. That's how I want it. I drink my wine undiluted.

SEPTEMBER 24

I have rented a room once again and am living as Engineer Malinovsky. I live as I like—without the rules of severe conspiracy. It doesn't matter to me now: let the police search for me; let them arrest me.

6. Annas was a high priest before whom Jesus was brought for judgment, prior to being brought before Pontius Pilate. Caiaphas was his son-in-law.

It's evening. It's cold. There's an illusive moon shining over the new factory chimney. The moonlight streams down on the roofs; the shadows stretch sleepily. The town's asleep. And I'm not asleep.

I'm thinking about Elena. I find it strange now that I could fall in love with her, and could kill in the name of love. I want to revive her kisses. Memory lies: there is no joy, no ecstasy. Words sound weary, hands caress lethargically. Love has been extinguished like an evening flame. Once more it's twilight, a monotonous life.

I ask myself: why did I kill? What did I accomplish by death? Yes, I believed that one could kill. But now I feel sad: I killed not only him; I also killed love. Sad autumn grieves as well: dead leaves are dropping. The dead leaves of my wasted days.

SEPTEMBER 25

By chance I got a newspaper today. I read in small print a piece from Petersburg:

Last night the police entered the Grand Hotel with a warrant for the arrest of Madame Petrova, a lady who resided there. In answer to a demand to open the door, a shot was heard. When the police broke in, they found the still-warm body of the suicide on the floor. An inquest has been launched.

It was Erna who was hiding at the hotel under the assumed name of Petrova.

SEPTEMBER 26

I know how it happened. At night, toward daybreak, they knocked at her door. It wasn't a loud knock. It was dark and quiet in the room. She was sleeping lightly and awoke at once. They knocked again, this time more insistently and louder. She hurriedly adjusted her hair and got up. Without turning on the light, she went barefoot to the large table on the right, near the piano. By feel, without making a sound, she pulled a revolver out of a drawer. I myself had given it to her. Then she started to get dressed, also feeling her way in the darkness. They knocked for the third and last time. Half-dressed, she went to a window in the corner. She pulled back the heavy curtain. She saw the stone courtyard, dry and narrow. Instead of stars, she saw the dim light of a lamp below. . . . They were already breaking down the door. Someone was steadily chopping at it with an axe. She turned toward the door, and with a strong, dexterous movement, pressed the revolver to her chest. Against her bare body. Near her heart, below her nipple. Then she lay on her back in the corner. The revolver was outlined in black on the carpet. Once again it was dark and quiet.

And now, at this very moment, I see her as if she were alive standing here at my door. Her hair is in disarray; her blue eyes are dim. Her frail body trembles as she whispers, "George, you'll come, won't you . . . George . . ."

Today I shall walk around Moscow. Crosses are gleaming on the churches. Bells are ringing gloomily for vespers. There's noise and conversation in the streets. Everything seems familiar and yet so distant. Here's the gate and here's the cross. It's here that Vanya killed. There in the lane below Fyodor died. I met Elena here. . . . Erna wept in the park. . . . It's all past. There had been a flame; now the smoke is dissipating.

SEPTEMBER 27

I'm bored with life. The days, weeks, and years stretch out monotonously. Today is like tomorrow and yesterday is like today. The same milky fog, the same grey everyday life. The same love, the same death. Life is like a narrow street: old houses, low, flat roofs, and factory chimneys. A black forest of stone chimneys.

It's a puppet show. The curtain has gone up, and we are on the stage. Pale Pierrot has fallen in love with Pierette.[7] He swears his eternal love. Pierette has a fiancé. A toy pistol fires and blood

7. Stock characters of pantomime and *commedia dell'arte* whose origins are in the late seventeenth-century Italian troupe of players performing in Paris.

flows—red cranberry juice. A street organ squeaks offstage. Curtain. The second scene: a hunt for a man. He's wearing a hat with a cock's feather, the admiral of the Swiss fleet. We have red mantles and masks. Rinaldo de Rinaldini is with us.[8] The carabineers pursue us. They can't catch us. The pistol fires again, the street organ squeaks. Curtain. The third scene: Here are Athos, Porthos, and Aramis, the three musketeers.[9] Their gilded jackets are sprinkled with wine. They hold cardboard swords in their hands. They drink, kiss, sing, and sometimes kill. Who's braver than Athos? Stronger than Porthos? Cleverer than Aramis? The finale. The street organ drones a fancy march.

Bravo. The gallery and the stalls are content. The actors have done their jobs. They're being dragged by their three-cornered hats, by their cock's feathers, and thrown into a box. The strings become tangled. Where's the admiral, Rinaldo, the enamored Pierette—who can figure it out? Good night. Until tomorrow.

Today I'm on the stage with Fyodor, Vanya, and the governor-general. Blood flows. Tomorrow they will drag me away. The carabineers are on the stage. Blood flows. In a week it will be the admiral, Pierette, and Pierrot again. And blood flows—cranberry juice.

Will people seek to make sense of it? And am I searching for links in the chain? And Vanya believes: in God? And Heinrich believes: in freedom? No, the world is simpler, of course. The tedious merry-go-round turns. People fly into the flame like moths. They perish in the fire. And does it really matter?

I'm bored. Day after day will race by again. The street organ will start to squeak off stage; Pierrot will be saved by his escape. Come. The farce is open to the public.

---

8. A literary figure from Christian August Vulpius's (1762–1827) novel *Rinaldo Rinaldini*, the robber's chief, who appeared in three volumes in Leipzig in 1798.

9. Characters from the historical adventure novel by Alexander Dumas (1802–1870) published in 1844.

I recall: one night in late autumn I was on the seashore. The sea was sighing sleepily, lazily creeping up on the beach, languidly washing the sand. There was a fog. In the white mournful mist all boundaries seemed to blend. The waves merged with the sky, the sand merged with the water. Something moist, watery, enfolded me. I didn't know where the end was, or the beginning; where the sea was, or the land. I breathed the salty moisture. I heard the rustling of the waves. There was not a star, not a bit of light. All around was transparent mist.

It's just like that now. There's no outline, no end or beginning. Is it vaudeville or drama? Cranberry juice or blood? A farce or real life? I don't know. Who does?

OCTOBER 1

I have fled Moscow. Yesterday evening I went to the station and mechanically took a seat on a train. The buffers clanged noisily, the springs bent. The engine whistled. Lights flashed hurriedly in the window. The wheels rattled swiftly.

There's autumn mud in Petersburg. The morning is gloomy. The waves in the Neva are like lead. There's a foggy shadow beyond the Neva, a sharp spire: the fortress.

At three o'clock the daylight fades and the lamps are lit. A howling wind comes from the sea. The Neva rebels against its granite banks: a flood.

It's boring. There are crosses in Moscow; in Petersburg there are soldiers. Monastery and barracks . . . I await nightfall. My hour comes at night. A time of oblivion and peace.

OCTOBER 3

Yesterday I happened to meet Andrei Petrovich on Nevsky Prospect. He was pleased to see me; his eyes smiled. He didn't approach me. Cautious, he followed me. I didn't want to see him. I didn't want to talk with him about business matters. I knew what he would say, his sensible sermons. I hastened my pace and turned into a lane. He caught up with me. "You've come back, George? Thank God." He shook my hand heartily. "Let's drop into a tavern."

As always, a damaged playing organ was squawking and waiters were scurrying about. I didn't like the tobacco smoke, the strong smell of vodka, food, and beer.

"We've been waiting for you, George."

"Well?"

He whispered mysteriously, "There's a great deal of work. . . . Have you heard—they came for Erna? She shot herself."

"Well?"

"The work must be organized. We've decided: the Minister of Justice." His grey beard was trembling; his eyes were blinking like an old man's eyes. He waited for my reply.

Pause. He said again, "We decided to entrust the job to you. It's difficult work: in Petersburg. But you'll manage it, George."

I listened to him but didn't really hear him. It was as if some stranger were speaking some strange words. Here he was summoning me to terror, once again to murder. I don't want to kill. What for?

And I said, "What for?"

"What do you mean, George?"

"Why kill?"

He didn't understand me; he poured a glass of cold water. "Drink. You're tired."

"I'm not tired."

"George . . . what's the matter with you?" He regarded me with alarm and affectionately stroked my hand like a father. But I knew already: I'm not with him, not with Vanya, nor with Erna. I'm with nobody.

I picked up my hat. "Goodbye, Andrei Petrovich."

"George . . ."

"Well?"

"George, you're not well: get some rest."

Pause. Then I said slowly, "I'm not tired and I am well. But I won't do anything more. Goodbye."

There was the same mud in the street; the same spire above the Neva. It's grey, damp, and miserable.

OCTOBER 4

I realized: I don't want to live any longer. I'm bored by my own words, my thoughts, and my desires. I'm bored with people, their life. There's a barrier between them and me. There are sacred boundaries. My boundary is a bloody sword.

I would look at the sun in my childhood. It would blind me, scorch me with its radiant light. In my childhood I felt love—maternal affection. I loved people innocently, loved life joyfully. Now I don't love anyone. I don't want to love and don't know how. The world is cursed and has become vacant for me in a single hour: it's all lies and vanity.

OCTOBER 5

There was the desire and I participated in the terror. I don't want to do it any longer. What for? For the stage? For the puppet show?

I recall: "He that loveth not, knoweth not God: for God is love."[10] I don't love and I don't know God. Vanya knew. Did he really know?

Furthermore: "Blessed are they that have not seen and yet have believed."[11] Believe in what? Pray to whom? I don't want the prayers of slaves. . . . Suppose Christ has illumined the world with His Word. I don't need serene light. Suppose love will save the world. I don't need love. I'm alone. I will leave the tedious puppet show. And if a temple opens its doors to me in heaven—even then I will say: it's all vanity and lies.

---

10. See above, p. 86.

11. John 20:29.

It's a clear and pensive day. The Neva is glittering in the sun. I love its majestic smoothness, the bed of its deep and still waters. The sad sunset dies in the sea; the purple skies are aflame. The waves splash sadly. The fir trees bend their tops. It smells of resin. When the stars come out, autumn night will fall, and I will say my last word: my revolver is with me.

SELECTED BIBLIOGRAPHY IN ENGLISH

Beer, Daniel. "The Morality of Terror: Contemporary Responses to Political Violence in Boris Savinkov's *The Pale Horse* (1909) and *What Never Happened* (1912)." *Slavic and East European Review* 85, no. 1 (January 2007): 25–46.

Churchill, Winston. "Boris Savinkov." In *Great Contemporaries*, 103–10. New York: G. P. Putnam's Sons, 1937.

Gamsa, Mark. "Savinkov and the Technique of Translation." In *The Chinese Translation of Russian Literature: Three Studies*, 49–106. Leiden: Brill, 2008.

Masaryk, Thomas. "The Crisis in Revolutionism; The Religious Question." In *The Spirit of Russia: Studies in History, Literature and Philosophy*, vol. 2, 435–61. Translated by Eden and Cedar Paul. London: Allen and Unwin, 1961–67.

Spence, Richard B. *Boris Savinkov: Renegade on the Left.* Boulder, CO: East European Monographs, 1991.

Wedziagolski, Karol S. *Boris Savinkov: Portrait of a Terrorist.* Translated by Margaret Patoski. Clifton, NJ: Kingston Press, 1988.